CW00816297

800 Years

a snippet into Christine's life
after her return from the Medieval England

by Ekaterina Crawford

The Ninth Gate Publishing

Books That Take You Places

Published by The Ninth Gate Publishing, 2020
Copyright © 2020 Ekaterina Crawford
Artwork and Cover design – Yennifer Ice

A CIP catalogue record for this book is available from British Library.

ISBNs:

Paperback: 978-1-912696-16-1
Kindle: 978-1-912696-15-4

The Ninth Gate Publishing
120 Baker St.,
London, W1U 6TU

www.ninthgatepublishing.co.uk

Author's Note and Acknowledgments:

First and foremost, I would like to thank those without who this book would not have been possible.

Yennifer Ice, thank you for our creative tandem. For your ability to feel my writing, to understand and catch the concept when I myself had only the faintest idea of what I want the cover of my story to look like. And of course, for your beautiful artwork!

Mimoza Abazi – my friend and work colleague – thank you for being my second pair of eyes and for making sure that all "a's" and "the' s" are in the right places! For fishing out all the silly typos and mistakes from the wild waterfalls of my first drafts.

Sue, Alison, Michelle and Pamela, for lending me your time and for being the best beta readers an aspiring author can dream of.

And a special thank you to Helen Setright and Roger Kirkpatrick, my dear friends and writing buddies from the Kingston Adult Education Centre. Thank you for your constructive criticism and for your guidance. Thank you for encouraging my writing and for always being a true inspiration!

Now to the business at hand.

What you have before you – a physical copy in your hands, or an e-copy on your device – was originally written to be a part of the second instalment of the Sherwood Untold trilogy – "Redemption". It was meant to bridge the first and the second parts of the second book and give a little inside into Christine's life, while Guy of Gisborne was fighting his demons back in medieval England.

It might still not have been the case, if COVID-19 had not messed things up. Working from home, schooling from home, trying not to go crazy at home and write at the same time had proven to be extremely difficult. So, I decided to publish Christine's part of the book as a separate story and get back to finishing the second instalment of the trilogy when life returns to its usual rhythm (as though it ever will!).

Don't feel disappointed that you won't find much of Guy of Gisborne in the story line of this piece, after all, this is a spin-off story dedicated to Christine. But whether or not the man in black leather is mentioned on the page, he's always in our thoughts and in our hearts.

Hope you enjoy the story.
Lots of love,

Ekaterina.

*"Tis better to have loved and lost
Than never to have loved at all."*

(Alfred Tennyson)

Making Amends

December 19, 2014
London

Mark leaned back in his chair and looked out of the window trying to refocus his vision.

Apart from a few brightly lit windows in the house on the other side of the road, the street was plunged into a late afternoon's gloom. The calendar was showing a few days left till Christmas, but the weather was still very warm, and a window of the flat on the fourth floor, opposite his office, was wide open, pouring out tunes of Christmas songs into the dark street.

In the window, moving to the rhythm of the melody, a young woman was cooking and laying out dinner. Navigating between the rooms, she appeared and disappeared from Mark's sight. She retreated into the kitchen and then appeared again with a large wicker basket covered with a white napkin and, for some time, stood by the table trying to find the best place for it. When something had disturbed her peaceful reflection, she placed the basket on the corner of the table and rushed out of the room.

When she re-appeared in Mark's view, she was no longer alone. Holding a huge bouquet of roses, she melted into her guest's embrace. Kissing hungrily, they dissolved into their passion. A moment later, the flowers were on the floor and they collapsed on the sofa.

"It could've been us…" Mark turned away from the window.

It's been nearly six months since Christine called off the engagement, and, although his bachelorhood was still an immensely enjoyable affair, at 38, more often than not, he found himself thinking about the comforts of family.

Mark pushed his chair away from his desk, rolled to the middle of the room and stretched out his tired limbs. He dropped his head back, closed his eyes, and, for some time, sat taking deep slow breaths.

"Everything could've been different..."

Suddenly, he jerked his eyes open and looked at the wall clock – it showed quarter to six. His gaze darted to the darkened screen of his computer. If he hurried up, he could still make it to his dad's within visiting hours. Not that he worried that hospital staff wouldn't have allowed Dr. Laferi to visit his dad outside the usual hours, but, if he was late, she wouldn't be there.

He rolled himself back to the table and wiggled the computer mouse. With a distinctive noise, the computer woke up. The screen lit up, revealing the notes on one of the patients Mark had seen earlier today. He focused on the text, scanning quickly through what he had typed up so far and, having caught his trail of thought, he lowered his fingers to the keyboard.

When he finished typing the notes, the wall clock showed five past six. The visiting hours at Royal Brompton ended at 7:30pm – if he left now, he should still be able to catch her there.

Loaded with work before Christmas, he hadn't seen Christine for almost two weeks. She never forgave him – not that he thought she would ever be able to, and that things would ever get back to the way they were before. He knew that their relationship would never be the same. Within the past few months, they had barely exchanged two dozen phrases, yet deep inside, the small embers of hope kept burning.

In a few clicks, Mark sent the document to print, and after the final read through, he signed the letter and placed it inside an envelope. He then turned off his PC, picked up his phone, car keys, the envelope, and his jacket, and exited his office.

His new secretary and PA – Rebecca – was at her desk. A full-bodied woman, Rebecca was a dramatic change from all of Mark's previous secretaries. With over 10 years' experience as a PA to one of London's wealthiest businessmen, she gladly accepted the offer from her HR agency, taking on the role of the office secretary and personal assistant to the prospering young doctor. Despite lacking experience in the medical sphere, she quickly got into the routine of the practice and, applying her professional skills, before long had managed to bring the administration of the clinic to proper order.

And even now, when everybody had long gone, she was still in the office, finishing up filing patient documents.

"I'm very sorry, but Dr. Laferi has already left the office," she said into the headset and winked at Mark as he walked in. "Of course, I understand, Mr. Bishop." At this name, Mark rolled his eyes. Rebecca smiled back. "Mr Bishop, I'm sure Dr. Laferi has not forgotten about your report. As a matter of fact," she added as Mark waved the envelope placed it on her desk, "your report is on my desk, at this very moment, and as soon as we finish our conversation, I will be happy to email you a copy. I can also post the original tomorrow morning, or, should you wish, you can pick it up on Monday, personally. Yes, I'll be at the clinic. No, Dr. Laferi won't be back until the 5th. Wonderful! Merry Christmas to you too, Sir. All the best," she finished and rang off.

"I'm amazed, how you can, so calmly, talk to that person," Mark said. "He drives me up the wall! His voice alone... makes me want to strangle him."

"Just a business etiquette," she responded, and walked to the big copier in the corner of the room.

She pressed the big green button and, for some time, patiently waited for the machine to come to life. Selecting the necessary mode, she lifted the cover and placed the letter on the glass surface, closed it and, once again, pressed the green button. The machine made a soft humming noise. For several seconds, the bright light shone up from under the cover of the scanner and then all went quiet. Rebecca returned to her desk. In a few swift clicks, she created a new email, quickly typed in the email address, wrote a few standard phrases, attached the scanned document, and pressed send. The mail program produced a sound as the mail was sent flying to its eagerly waiting recipient. Rebecca moved the computer mouse to the side, folded her hands in front of her and lifted her eyes up to Mark.

"And that is done!"

"Thank you, I don't know what I would do without you, Rebecca."

"It's my pleasure, Sir. You are a wonderful doctor, I'm just helping to make your important work easier," she said. "Leaving already?"

"Yes, I wanted to visit Dad, haven't been there lately."

"Haven't you now?" she asked with a smile. "Weren't you there yesterday?"

"Yes, I was but I have not seen–,"

"Your father?" she squinted at him, still smiling.

Mark lowered his eyes in embarrassment.

"Your lady-friend, the barrister?" she smiled again.

"Yes," he answered, still a little embarrassed. "Christine. I haven't seen her for 2 weeks. Wanted to catch up and invite her to the Christmas party. Speaking of Christmas–,"

"No need to worry, doctor, everything is under control. I'll be here on Monday and then on the 29th and the 30th."

"Are you sure you don't want to take some time off? See your family?"

"No, it's alright. They are going on holidays on Christmas Eve, and won't be back until the New Year's."

"Very well, let me know if you change your mind. Your wages for December will be paid on the 2nd," he said, handing her an envelope and added, "and this is for you. A small token of my appreciation. Merry Christmas!"

"Oh! It's very kind of you, but you shouldn't have, doctor!" she said smiling shyly. "I, also, have something for you," she said removing from her bag a red envelope decorated with tinsel and glitter. "Happy Christmas, doctor."

"What is it?" Mark asked surprised.

"It's a card! A Christmas card," she laughed.

"Oh! Thanks! How thoughtful of you. I'm touched," Mark said stowing the card away in a pocket of his jacket. "If you don't mind, I'll open it on Christmas Day."

"Of course, Sir."

"To tell the truth, none of my previous secretaries ever gave me a Christmas card."

"I'm sure they gave you something very different for Christmas..." she gave him the look.

"Ha! Right!" Mark burst out laughing. "Thank you very much, once again. If you change your mind and would have nothing to entertain yourself with on Christmas Eve, I'd be happy to see you at the Dorchester," he said and headed for the door.

"Thank you, doctor, I'll think about it. Happy Christmas!"

"Merry Christmas!" he cried over his shoulder and exited the office.

A few moments later he was descending the stairs, a few steps at the time.

*****

He drove past Wellington Arch and turned left. Cutting corners through small, one-way traffic streets, he entered Knightsbridge. Chelsea in the evening sparkled and shone with the lights of hotels and luxury boutiques. Locals and tourists, who came to London to celebrate Christmas and New Year's, moved in some version of Brownian motion, hurrying from one boutique to another, balancing heavy packages and countless bags with presents and souvenirs in their hands.

Waiting in the traffic by Harrods, Mark noted an Arabian family: a man in his early sixties, dressed in colourful national clothes of his country, and three female figures wrapped by the long fabric of their burkas. Passionately waving their hands about, the four of them were having a fiery conversation. Mark couldn't understand the words but, judging by the tone, their articulation and the quick glances towards a window display filled with designer handbags, the head of the family was trying to talk his women out of investing in another needless accessory. Unfortunately for him, the battle was lost and, cursing in his native language, the man followed the ladies into the bright and glittering iridescent rainbow of colours of the mousetrap called "Harrods".

"That'll be one expensive Christmas," Mark chuckled.

The colours of the traffic light went through the whole cycle, but his car hadn't moved an inch. He sighed, and resting his hands on the steering wheel, waited through another cycle. On the second attempt, the car in front of him started the engine and moved forward, but having just crossed the box, stopped in another traffic jam. Mark drove to the lights and stopped – the road after the junction was completely blocked.

The evening was shimmering with the soft silver and gold glimmer of Christmas lights, but despite all the trees, garlands and various Christmas installations, Mark did not feel festive, hoping it all might change after he spoke with Christine.

He turned on the radio, flicked through the various stations that broadcasted the same compilation of Christmas songs, and switched to the news channel. Absently listening to the monotonous voice of the radio presenter, he floated far away in his thoughts, watching the kaleidoscope of lights slowly changing before his eyes.

Soon the radio played the chime, signalling the start of a new hour. He looked at his watch – he'd been sitting in this gridlock for nearly thirty minutes. If he could not get to the hospital within the next ten-fifteen minutes, he would, most certainly, miss her again.

"C'mon, c'mon! Move!" he muttered, irritated, and as if obeying, the cars on the opposite side of the intersection began to move.

*****

By the time he arrived at the Royal Brompton his watch showed a quarter past seven. Among the cars still parked outside the hospital, he saw Christine's Mini. Mark parked next to it and patted the Mini's bonnet. He threw his doctor's badge around his neck and hurried inside.

Trying to hold back the silly smile of a little boy who had concocted a daring plan, he entered the building, greeted the hospital staff at the front reception and walked, immediately, towards the stairs, knowing too well that if she were leaving, she, most certainly, wouldn't use the lift.

Conquering a few steps at a time, he rushed up to the third floor. Entering the bright ward from the dim lights of the stairwell, he was blinded for a moment and collided with one of his friends and colleagues – Rupinder Singh.

Rupinder – a third generation Sikh, whose family immigrated to the UK at the beginning of the twentieth century, was an amazing example and keeper of the national traditions of his ancestors. Translated into English, his name meant the "greatest beauty" and it matched him perfectly. Taller than the average Sikh, he was well-built with wide shoulders, strong hands and beautiful, dark-honey coloured, almond-shaped eyes. His head was always tightly wrapped in a black turban, beard, and moustache elegantly styled. He and Mark had known each other for some years now and had often met in the operating theatre.

"Mark?" Rupinder exclaimed, struggling to stay upright. "What are the chances! What are you doing here?"

"Hey, Rup! Is she still here?" Mark asked, fighting for his breath.

"Who?"

Mark gave his colleague a long look. Rupinder lowered his eyes, a blush of embarrassment appeared on his dark skin.

"Yes. She is still with your dad."

"Thanks mate," Mark patted Rupinder on the shoulder and hurried towards his dad's room.

A few meters from the room he stopped, trying to steady his pounding heart; was it from the quick run up the stairs or in anticipation of seeing her, Mark wasn't sure.

She was here. She was close – closer than she had been in the past few months. He could see her through the window. In the dimmed light of the room she was sitting by his father's bed, holding his hand, gently. Her lips were moving, from time to time curving into a soft, little smile, but her gaze was fixed on Philip's face, who was lying calm and quiet in his bed. It had been five months since the last operation, and he had yet to wake up.

Mark waited for another few moments, allowing his heart to calm and return to its usual rhythm, then wiped his sweaty palms on his trousers and entered the room.

She heard the noise and turned at the sound but noting who had disturbed her private conversation with Philip, she turned away and shot a quick glance at her watch.

"Hello," Mark said.

"Hey there," she answered drily.

He walked closer and laid a gentle hand on her shoulder. Christine's eyebrow arched, as she lowered her gaze to his hand.

"Sorry. Old habits die hard," he laughed, a little awkwardly, and withdrew his hand.

"It's time to make new habits. Perhaps," she said in the same unfriendly tone.

She was still angry with him, he was certain of that. It'd been a long time, but she hadn't forgiven him. Over the past months, he had never gotten a chance to sit and talk with her, to put things right. She didn't want that and avoided him at every opportunity.

"How is he?" Mark asked.

"Shouldn't I be asking you?" she lifted her eyes at him questioning, and then suddenly got up, picking up her jacket from a chair. "I'll leave you to it," she said coldly and added in a very soft tone as she turned to Philip. "I'll see you in a few days. Love you."

She bent over the bed and kissed the dry parchment of his cheek and headed for the door.

"Hey, you don't need to leave on my account," Mark caught her hand.

"You think too much of yourself, Mark," she said. "I've been here for nearly two hours, it's time for me to go home. Besides, visiting hours have already finished and, unlike some, I don't own a staff badge."

"Are you alright?" Mark asked, as she reached for the door handle.

"Everything is perfect!" she said, putting on a theatrical smile.

"I don't think so," he said, noting the dark circles under her eyes.

"Does it look like I care what you think? Good evening!"

She exited the room, quickly walked to the door on the other side of the hall and disappeared behind it. Mark caught up with her on the ground floor.

"Are you sure you are alright?"

"I thought I already answered that question." she stopped at the entrance of a small coffee shop and looked at him – her big sky-blue eyes were cold. Looking at her now, he remembered, how many times before these eyes had looked at him with love and passion, smiling happily.

"Yes, of course... it's just you don't look very..."

"Why does it bother you how the hell I look, Mark?" she turned around and walked to the counter. "Double espresso, please."

"Espresso? At this hour? Have you gone mad?"

She glared at him and turned back to the woman at the counter.

"Double espresso. Please," she repeated.

"No!" protested Mark. Picking up a bottle of fresh fruit juice, he handed it to the woman. "This, please."

"What the hell, Mark!" She threw her hands up and she turned to him.

In the bright light of the hall the dark circles under her eyes looked almost purple and only now he noticed her sunk in cheeks. She looked exhausted – exhausted and angry.

"I just want..."

"You just want to leave me alone, alright? I have enough to deal with. Without you," she turned away and addressed the lady at the counter once again. "How about my coffee?"

Mark made a quick sign to the woman, and, carefully taking Christine by the elbow, walked her to the side.

"What do you think you are doing?" she jerked her hand back.

"Alright, alright. Calm down, please?"

"What do you want from me?" she asked angrily.

"I just want to talk with you."

"And I don't! Is that so difficult to understand?" She tried to walk around him.

"You don't need to be like this, Christine."

"Like what?" She glared at him again.

"A bitch! All right?" he blurted out. "It's not you!"

"Really? Perhaps, you don't know me. And never did!" she shouted. "Forget about the coffee," she said to the lady and hurried away from the cafeteria.

"Christine, we need to talk. How much longer will you be avoiding me?"

"Till the end of time sounds about right."

He caught up with her and tried to stop her, but Christine pushed him away.

"Is everything alright, doctor?" asked one of the passing by members of the hospital stuff.

"Yes. Everything's under control," Mark assured her, not taking his eyes off Christine.

"Everything is grand!" Christine said in a raised voice. "Former lovers' quarrel. You should mind your own business."

The volume of their conversation started to attract the attention of other people in the hospital – one of the doctors peeked from his room, two others watched the scene playing out before them from the far end of the hallway.

Rupinder, also making use of his fifteen-minute break, came down to the cafeteria and found his friend arguing loudly with his ex-fiancée.

"Mark, you still here? I heard voices from the stairs... Good evening, Miss," his smile was barely noticeable and for a long moment his eyes lingered upon her face.

"What are you staring at?" she gave him a look.

"Christine, there is no need to be rude," Mark made another attempt to take her hand.

"Who are you to tell me what I should and shouldn't do?"

"Christy, we need to talk. Let's go outside or into a room," Mark took her hand, directing her towards one of the empty rooms.

Christine jerked her hand back.

"Mark? Is everything alright?" Rupinder asked cautiously, his eyes darting between Mark and Christine.

"Don't worry, he'll handle it. Mentally unstable women are his specialty," Christine sneered. "By the way, shouldn't you be going somewhere? Don't you have patients to attend to?"

"We don't need to make a scene in public. Everyone is watching," Mark said, attempting to reason.

"I don't care! Let them watch if they have nothing else to entertain themselves with. I have nothing to talk about with you," she snapped. "Good day!"

"Christy..."

"Go to hell, Mark!" she cried, walking away from him.

"Christine, we need to talk," Mark caught up with her again.

"How many times do I have to repeat? I. Don't. Want. To talk. With you!"

"Stop it, Christine!" Mark flipped. "How many times would I have to apologise–,"

"Oh, I pity you, Mark!" she shook her head. "You really think that the world revolves around you, don't you? Do you really think I have nothing else to think about?"

Mark noticed that she tried to look indifferent but deep inside her something trembled. He was sure that his colleague had noticed that too. Rupinder opened his mouth to speak but, Mark stopped him, lifting his hand.

"If it wasn't for you..." she whispered.

"Philip? Are you worried about him? He'll be fine! You know it. I know it. We just need to wait for his body to get stronger–,"

"If it was not for you..." she repeated, her voice was breaking, tears began to gather in her eyes.

"If it wasn't for me," the harsh words bounced off his lips too quickly, "if it wasn't for me, he wouldn't have survived the injury!"

Christine gasped. Her face changed – an insufferable pain distorted her beautiful features. His words, like a sharp knife, cut deep into a wound, he knew that. He regretted saying that, but a word is not a bird. What has been said, cannot be unsaid.

She looked at him, tears flowing from her eyes. She tried to speak, to say something back, to hurt him, as he, just now, had hurt her. Again. But breathless, she could not utter a word.

"I hate you!" she mumbled finally. "I hate–,"

She didn't finish. Turning pale, she stumbled to the side. Mark and Rupinder rushed forward but failed to catch her.

*****

The sharp pain brought her back to reality. She felt a sting and then the heat of flames slowly began to run through her veins. With a heavy moan, she opened her eyes. The light blinded her, everything seemed doubled and blurred. It smelled as well. A smell of spirit and medicine. Of a hospital.

"What happened..." she mumbled. "Where am I?"

"Shh, it's all right," said an unfamiliar voice.

Christine turned towards the sound. She was laying on a blue hospital bed, a plastic tube was attached to her vein. A transparent liquid dripped into the tube and slowly ran down to her arm.

Next to her bed stood a tall man in blue scrubs and a black turban. He took her hand, his cold fingers held tight to the inside of her wrist. He was quiet for some time, measuring the beat, then lowered her hand, wrote something on a piece of paper attached to the note board in his hands and exited the room.

Behind the curtain that separated Christine from the rest of the ward, she heard muffled voices.

"I need to speak with her," whispered the first voice.

"Don't think it's a very good idea," answered another.

The man in the turban, Christine thought. She closed her eyes and, in her memory, tried to reproduce his face. Apart from two bright patches – blue of the uniform and black of the turban – she couldn't remember anything.

"... you saw how your first attempt to speak with her ended. Let her be. I'll check if we can find her a bed for the night. She needs rest."

"Not sure she will be willing to stay," chuckled the first voice. This time it was louder.

"Mark?!"

"We'll see about that. You stay here, I'll go and check about the bed," said the second voice. "Don't bother her!" it added in a stricter tone.

She heard retreating steps and then everything went quiet. She spent some time, aimlessly looking about the room and then gathered all her strength and lifted herself on one elbow.

"Mark," she called. "Mark, I know you're there!" she called again, this time louder.

There was a motion on the other side, a sigh of hesitation and then a familiar face peered from behind the curtain.

"Hey! How are you?" Mark asked stepping into her cubicle.

"What happened?"

"You fainted," he said, sitting himself on the side of her bed. "To tell the truth, I freaked out a little when you collapsed on the floor all of a sudden. One moment you were shouting at me and in the next you were laying on the floor in the middle of the hallway. But, to be honest I'm glad it happened, I was beginning to worry that you might punch me in the nose. Again."

He smiled widely, rubbing the little bump on his nose. Christine smiled too, involuntarily. For some time, they looked at one another not saying a word, then, carefully, Mark took her hand in his.

"You really scared me. If it was not for Rup," he nodded towards the hallway, separated from them by the blue curtain. "Nice guy, by the way. Head over heels with you. Desperately in love." Christine's eyes widened. "I'm serious! He even asked to change his shift to see you more often."

"To see me more often?"

"Sure. You are here every day, visiting dad and he is lurking in the shadows of the corridors, admiring you from afar," Mark smiled, moving his eyebrows up and down.

"Oh God! The last thing I need right now," she mumbled under breath and laid herself back on the pillow.

The curtain flew open and a tall man in a black turban entered the cubicle.

"I knew you wouldn't listen!" he said shooting a strict glance at Mark. "Right, have you looked at her? Spoken with her? Now, please, out. I need to speak with Miss Hawk alone."

"Is it something serious?" Mark asked, worried.

"None of your business. Out of here. Please."

"Rup, please, doctor to doctor –,"

"Out! Unless you're an emergency contact. Which I seriously doubt."

"It's ok, he can stay," Christine said.

"As a matter of fact, I am her "call to" in case of emergency," Mark said proudly.

"Should've changed that," Christine swore quietly and added, "he's like a brother to me."

"What?!" Mark exclaimed. "That's a punch below the belt! If we were brother and sister, some of the things we have done, would've been illegal."

"Mark!" Christine snapped. "I don't think doctor..." she paused, struggling to read a name on his badge. Blushing deeply under his beard, Rupinder turned the badge to her. "Doctor Singh," she said, finally making up the writing through her blurred vision, "would not be interested in knowing the details of our relationship. What's happened to me, doctor?"

"You fainted," he said, a little shyly.

"That I understood from your colleague over there," Christine nodded in Mark's direction. "Fainting is the result. What caused it?"

"Your blood pressure dropped," said Rupinder.

"Low blood pressure?" Mark repeated alarmed. "How low?"

"60/40. We're waiting for the blood test results, yet I'm 99% certain that, together with her blood pressure, her sugar levels dropped as well."

"Hypo?" Mark asked concerned.

"Too early to say, but by the looks of it..." Rupinder said, surveying the drip attached to Christine's vein. He carefully picked up her wrist, found her pulse and for a quarter of a minute stood motionless, measuring the rhythm. Making a note in his paper, he looked at the almost empty drip and closed the vent.

"Congratulations! Well done you!" Mark shook his head disapprovingly.

"Hypo? What's that?" Christine asked quietly.

"I need to ask you something," Rupinder ignored her question. "But I need you to be completely honest with me."

"Yes, of course," she answered, a little absently.

"When was the last time you ate?"

"Today, at lunch. Why do you ask?"

"And by "ate" I mean normal human food, not coffee, crisps and chocolate."

"Ehm..." Christine lifted her eyes up to the ceiling, in a failing attempt to remember. "Wednesday evening..." she said, not sounding very convincing.

"And if you think a little more?" he asked her again, there was no escape from him.

"Tuesday. Lunch."

"Tuesday?" Mark exclaimed. "Have you gone completely mad?

"Oh, don't shout, please," Christine moaned. "My head hurts as it is."

"Have you decided to starve yourself to death?"

"I was busy, alright. And please stop shouting! Or better, go and sit outside."

"She's right, Mark, you'd better leave. I'm finishing now. We'll take her upstairs and you can argue there to your heart's content."

"Upstairs?" Christine stared at the doctor.

"I want to keep you here for a few days, keep an eye on your blood pressure and then on Monday, if all is well, you can go home."

"No! I'm not staying!" she protested and tried to get off the bed. Dizzy at the attempt, she lowered herself back to the pillow. "Mark, please," she looked at Mark.

"Perhaps, it's for the best," he ignored her plea.

"I can't stay here!"

"Why not? What holds you?" Mark smirked. "Family, young children? And here you will be under supervision."

"I. I need to finish something. For work," she tried again.

"Christy, it's the nineteenth of December, Christmas is in five days. I hardly believe you'll have any hearings before the New Year."

"Mark!"

"What?"

"I'm fine, I'm just tired!"

24

"Exactly. You need rest. Stay here for a few days, recharge and go back to the world good as new."

"Mark, please, I can't stay here," she begged. "Please..."

"Rup, can I speak with you for a moment?" Mark said. There was something in her pleading eyes that softened him.

"Yes, of course," said Rupinder, looking slightly confused, and followed Mark out of the cubicle.

"How bad is it?" Mark asked, trying to speak as quietly as possible.

"It's not life threatening. Yet. But she is exhausted. And dehydrated. All those coffees... Don't think, I need to explain it to you, do I? She needs rest and sleep, lots of liquids and proper food."

"Yes, of course. I understand," Mark said, thoughtful. "Listen, let her go. Discharge her, I'll take all responsibility, of course. I'll speak with her today... although I'm sure she understands. She's a clever girl. It's been a few long and difficult months for her. My dad is upstairs," he nodded towards the ceiling, "her work is very stressful, everything just piled up..."

"Mark, I honestly, don't think it's a good idea."

"Rup, please..." Mark looked at him making a face like an innocent child.

"Oh, almighty Waheguru! Alright! Just don't look at me like that. Ever again! Or I'll punch you in the face," he laughed.

"Thanks, buddy!" Mark patted him on the shoulder.

"Under your responsibility," Rupinder said. Mark waived him off, already slipping into the cubicle.

"What?" Christine asked, worried. "What did he say?"

"He said you will need to stay here till Monday."

"What? I can't! You know I can't..." Christine protested but, seeing his lips stretch into a smug grin, changed her tone. "You, bastard!" she uttered and, gathering all her strength, drew a pillow from under her head and threw it at Mark.

"Sorry, I couldn't resist, you should've seen your face!"

"It's not funny."

"Yes. I'm sorry."

"So, what did the doctor... what's his name... say?"

"Rup? He said he will let you go today, but only on one condition."

"What condition?" she asked, sitting up.

"That you have a dinner with me today."

"Did he now..." Christine smiled.

"Well, he didn't phrase it exactly like that. He said he'll let you go under my supervision and responsibility. And that I make sure you eat."

"I guess I don't have any other option but to agree?" Christine mumbled, smiling.

"Exactly so!" he nodded approvingly. "Come."

Mark helped her from the bed. She picked up her bag and jacket and, leaning onto his arm for support, walked out of the cubicle. Together, they walked to his car.

"But my..." she protested, when Mark guided her to the passenger door of his car, opening it for her.

"Don't worry, I'll pick it up tomorrow morning. You shouldn't be driving today."

"I'll be clamped! Some, unlike you, don't have a badge for staff parking."

"Don't trouble yourself with that," Mark said, helping her into the car.

He fastened her seatbelt, closed her door, and quickly walked back to the hospital building. Through the glass doors, of the brightly lit hall, Christine saw him talking with the girl at the reception and the security guard. He looked back a few times and showed the guard his badge. They talked for a few moments longer and then, having received a piece of paper from the lady at the reception, Mark wrote something quickly, shook the guard's hand and walked out. Leisurely, he strolled to her car and stuck the piece of paper under the wipers of the Mini.

"That's sorted," he smiled, got into the car, and started the engine.

*****

Half an hour later, they were sitting in a small Italian restaurant, at a table by the window.

"Let me know when you are ready to order," said the waiter, placing open menus before them.

"Yes, of course," Mark said with a friendly smile, and lowered his eyes to the cocktail list. "Please, do not go. Can we have two of these, two of these and one this one, please," he said tracing his finger over the names of the drinks.

"Should I bring everything at the same time?" asked the waiter, not at all surprised.

"No, bring some water to start with, then this with the starter and this with the main course."

"Starter and a main course?" Christine asked, surprised, as soon as the waiter departed to register their order at the till.

"Of course! And a dessert as well!" replied Mark, not looking up at her.

Adopting a serious face, he carefully studied the content of the menu.

"Oh, stop staring into that!" Christine laughed, snatching the large piece of thick, ivory-coloured paper decorated with golden monograms, from his hands. "We've been here so many times, you probably know it by heart," she added, but as quickly as the smile lit up her face, it disappeared without a trace.

Mark didn't say anything and called the waiter. While he was giving their order, Christine was quiet and totally oblivious to the names of her favourite dishes, dictated by Mark to the waiter. She looked out of the window absently. Her body was there, but her soul seemed to have flown millions and millions of miles away, to a different reality. She didn't even notice as the waiter had brought a bottle of water, filled their glasses and retreated again, to serve other customers.

Drifting far away in her thoughts she watched as, beyond the invisible barrier of the glass, life, brightened by colourful Christmas lights, went on as usual.

She blinked a few times and shook her head, chasing away the thoughts she was floating in, when the waiter appeared once again and placed the plates with the starters on the table and a strawberry Margarita before her.

"Mmm," she murmured quietly and reached for her favourite drink.

"Not so fast, lovely," Mark tapped her hand slightly and covered the top of the glass with his palm. "Water first, then some food and after that a cocktail."

"Doctor's orders," she smiled, a little laboured but took the glass offered to her by Mark and drank a half of it.

Mark moved a plate with melon and Italian ham in front of her and watched as three pieces of fruit wrapped in Parma quickly disappeared from her plate.

"That's a good girl!" he said satisfied and removed the hand covering her drink.

She brought the glass up to her lips and took a few sips, leaning back in her chair.

"Do not forget to eat," Mark smiled, watching as she slowly sipped the cocktail. "I promised Rup I would feed you, not get you drunk."

They exchanged a few more pleasantries and finished the remainder of their starters in silence.

"I missed this place," she said suddenly, when the waiter replaced their empty plates with the next set of drinks and the main course.

"Yes. You always loved it here."

"Brings back memories."

"Good memories, I hope?" asked Mark and reached his glass out to her.

"All kinds of..." she answered wearily and lightly clinked her glass against his. She sipped the cocktail and looked out of the window, her gaze becoming empty and absent, once again.

"Christine?" Mark called softly, but she didn't respond. He reached out to her and she flinched in surprise, as he touched her hand. "Where are you disappearing to all the time?" he asked, trying to make his words to sound like a joke.

"Nowhere," she said, attempting to smile. "I'm here."

"Doesn't look like it. I mean, you're here with me, but sometimes you seem to be a million miles away."

"It does not matter. I'm here. Now."

Mark felt as the tension began to rise. Not wishing to provoke a repeat of the afternoon's events, he changed the subject.

"The past few months have worn me out so much, that I can't wait for the Christmas break," he said, picking up his glass and leaning back in his chair.

"That doesn't sound like you at all," Christine smiled faintly. "You always hated Christmas."

"Yeah, I'm getting sentimental," he drawled and took another long sip of his drink.

"You mean you're getting old!" Christine laughed, and it was exactly the moment Mark had been waiting for.

"So, how have you been all this time?" he asked leisurely, as if he was not at all interested in her response.

"Fine. I guess," she said, once again, taking a defensive position.

"Really? Don't believe it for the world. Were you exhausting yourself with work too? When was the last time you looked at yourself in the mirror?"

"This morning. Why?"

"This morning? Yeah, right. And what did you see there?"

"Nothing unusual, eyes, a nose and a of pair of lips, like everyone else."

"Like everyone else," Mark repeated, mimicking her tone. "If I didn't know you, I would never have guessed it was you. You look terrible!"

"Oh, thanks, Mark!" she chuckled. "You always knew how to compliment a woman," she added as a light blush coloured her face.

"Always welcome!" he said with passion." If not me, who else would tell you?"

"I have a lot on my plate," she said, a little defensive.

"I can see that! Literally!" he laughed, lowering his eyes to her plate. Her main course still untouched. She smiled as well.

"Your dad, my work and..." she trailed off. "Many other things," she said, her face suddenly changing.

"My dad will be fine, don't worry about him. He's my responsibility. You need to think about yourself, relax, recharge, have sex, for Christ sake," he said and moved his eyebrows up and down playfully.

"Are you offering me your services?" she asked trying to hold back the smile.

"I'm always happy to help, to the best of my abilities... when a friend is in need," he clarified, his lips stretching into a wide grin.

"Sex is the last thing on my mind right now," she said dryly, her good mood evaporated.

"That's awfully bad! And this I say as a doctor," he moved the martini closer to her. "Look, I have the most splendid idea, why don't you come to our party? My colleagues and I've rented a hall in the Dorchester for Christmas Eve. Cost us an arm and a leg, but a great place. Come, it'll be fun!"

"Why, thank you for the invitation but, right now, I'm not the best company for social events. Besides, I'm not in the best form."

"Oh, come on! Don't say that. You do look terrible, that's for sure, but your forms... I mean, they're really, really and I do mean really good," he looked at her lustfully.

"Oh, stop it," she smiled.

"That's much better!" Mark said sensing the change in her mood. "I'm serious! Come."

"Thank you. But no, thank you."

"Oh, c'mon! Please," he made the most innocent face and folded his hands on his chest in prayer. "Please."

"No!" laughed Christine. The cocktails began to take their relaxing effect.

"Pretty please," Mark said, moving his chair away from the table. "I can get down on my knees..." he added, immediately putting words into action.

"Get up! What are you doing, people are watching!" She looked around, her eyes darting from one side of the restaurant to the other, as if looking for help and support from the other customers.

"Let them watch, they don't bother me. Pretty please," he murmured and put the most charming smile on his face.

Christine smiled, shaking her head. Mark picked up the martini from the table, snatched the toothpick with the olives and lifted it above his head. Christine frowned, not understanding his gesture.

"Well, there're no cherries available," Mark said as a matter of fact.

"You're mad!" Christine chuckled, still looking around.

"Is that a yes, then?"

"You're mad!" she laughed again, and she saw a familiar face – a doctor in a black turban – at the entrance door, she energetically waived her hand. "Doctor Singh! How fortunate! I think your colleague here needs some medical help."

She was still laughing as Rupinder made his way to their table.

"Mark, are you alright?" Rupinder asked, confused.

"Yep, everything is fine, Rup," Mark said looking up at him. "I'm trying to persuade this lovely young lady to come to our party," he added, still on his knees.

"Really?" the doctor's eyes lit up. "Will you really come?"

Still laughing, Christine shook her head negatively.

"See, I didn't get too far with it. Yet. I think together we'll have a better chance," he said and pulled his colleague down.

"Stop it, both of you!" Christine's happy laugh echoed through the restaurant. "Alright! I will come."

"Perfect!" Mark said satisfied, getting to his feet, and returning to his chair. "You finished already?" he asked his colleague.

"Yes, wanted to get something to eat before going back home."

"Good! Join us," Mark suggested. "We'll get a bigger table. Right?" he turned to Christine.

"I don't mean to disturb you," Rupinder said, feeling a little awkward.

"No-no, by all means, join us," Christine said, looking grateful to him for freeing her from yet another series of Mark's questions that caused her so much discomfort.

*****

Mark stopped the car a few meters from Christine's house and killed the engine. For some time, they sat in silence.

"Thank you," Christine said. "Thank you for this evening."

"My pleasure. Glad that you had a nice time."

"Yes," she breathed out quietly, "You're right, Rupinder really is a nice guy."

"Told you, a really nice fella," Mark smiled, "and allow me to remind you, head over heels in love with you. Maybe you will reconsider," he gave her a meaningful look.

"I appreciate your concern, but no."

"Why not? I'm serious by the way. You need some distraction. Relax, go somewhere. Or even better! He's a cracking cook! Makes the most amazing curries I have ever tasted in my life, and you look like you have not eaten for a month."

"Thanks!" Christine laughed involuntary. "Another compliment."

"Always welcome!"

"In case you've forgotten, I hate curries."

"Well then, forget about the curry, just go to the movies or something. Have fun, no strings attached. And you won't be alone…"

"I'll be under doctor's supervision you meant to say," Christine corrected him.

"My sentiments exactly!" Mark clicked his tongue and winked. "And he'll go out with the girl of his dreams. Win-win."

He got out from the car, walked around it, and opened the passenger door.

"Mademoiselle," he bowed, waving his hand in an old-fashioned gesture, inviting her out of the car.

She chuckled softly, reached for his hand, and jumped out. He held her by the elbow and together they slowly walked to her house. She pulled out the keys and was about to open the door when Mark stopped her.

"Wait," he said, in a tone, not at all usual for him. "I need to say something."

"Don't," in the darkness of the street he could see as her face tensed.

"No, I need to," he interrupted her. "I'm glad everything turned out as it did today. The hospital and the rest… I finally got a chance to speak with you."

"Mark. Please."

He didn't listen. The last few days he'd been preparing himself for this conversation and he didn't mean to back off now.

"I should've said it before, but I was a coward... I'm sorry," he said looking into her eyes. "I was a stupid fool and, when I see how I wronged you, how much pain I've caused you and dad..."

"Don't, please... it's all in the past," she said trying to put on a brave face. "Besides, you yourself said your dad will be fine."

"Yes, he'll be fine, but I hurt YOU," he softly touched her cheek removing a stray lock from her face. "When I see you so... it's just not you! It's like you're fading away... I can't bear it."

"It's not you, Mark," she said with a deep sigh. "I–,"

"Perfect! Then, you wouldn't mind if I pop in for a glass of... tea?"

"I don't think it's a particularly good idea. I think I drank too much to invite you in, even for a cup of tea."

"Well, that was my plan exactly!" he added cheerfully.

"It didn't work," she shook her head, barely able to hold back her smile.

"Damn! All those cocktails for nothing!"

"Night Mark," she said turning to the door.

"Rest well."

He held her hand, not letting her go. His fingers touched her cheek softly and slid slowly down her face, tracing her neck, and stopping at her shoulder. He drew a sharp breath, moving his face closer to hers. Christine turned away, avoiding his kiss – his lips brushing against her cheek.

"Don't complicate something that is already complicated," she said quickly and disappeared behind the door.

Mark wanted to say something, but instead just lifted his hand and waved goodbye to the closed door. He returned to the car and, with a loud squeal of the tires over the wet tarmac and loud roar of his car's engine, disappeared into the darkness of the night.

*****

For a long time after walking into the house, Christine stood in the dark hall leaning against the front door, listening to her heart hammering inside her chest. Everything that she had tried to ignore, to avoid these past long months, had descended upon her. She'd known that sooner or later she would have to face him and that sooner or later Mark would try to speak with her, but, as it turned out, she had not been at all ready.

Did she forgive him? No. Would she ever be able to forgive him? She didn't know. She was still angry, yet she did not know what angered her more – his betrayal and the way he treated her, or how their break up and her disappearance caused Philip's fall or that because of it, she had to leave Guy. Her heart began to ache again, the lump was building inside her throat, robbing her of breath. The events of the past summer seemed to be so far away, but still very vivid in her memory.

She didn't move until the sound of Mark's car faded away in the distance. It took her some time to calm down, but once she managed that, she turned on the lights and took off her shoes. Leaving her jacket in the hall on a small stand by the mirror, she walked into the kitchen and turned on the kettle.

Slowly she climbed up the stairs and, relieving herself of her remaining clothes went straight into the shower.

Some fifteen minutes later, she got out of the shower feeling considerably better. She changed into long flannel trousers, a light cami and a top with a zip, put on warm knitted socks and went downstairs. The kettle has long boiled and filled the kitchen with hot moist air. Christine took a mug and placed it on the counter. Then took a jar of coffee and, without giving it a second thought, measured three spoons of the brown granular substance into her mug. She put the jar away and was about to pour some hot water into her cup when she heard the soft buzzing of the phone coming from the hall.

"Hello?" she asked, a little cautious. She usually didn't answer to unknown numbers but, thinking the call might be from the hospital, pressed the green button on the screen.

"I hope you're not drinking coffee," the voice said on the other side.

"Are you spying on me?" she smiled.

"No, I just know you too well," said Mark.

"Did you hide your number on purpose then?"

"Of course! You would've never picked up knowing it is me. Although, after this evening... so coffee?"

"No," Christine lied.

"That's my girl!"

"Good night Mark," she said and dropped the call.

She returned to the kitchen and looked at the mug with coffee granules. She smiled at her thoughts as she put the coffee back into its jar, put the washed mug on the kitchen counter and began to rummage through the contents of the vegetables box of her fridge.

"Come out, come out wherever you are," she mumbled.

She couldn't find what she was looking for, so she closed the fridge, took a step back and leaned against the counter. The coffee jar was still standing next to the kettle, seducing by its closeness.

Determined to find what she was looking for, she opened the fridge door once again, immediately finding a lonely, slightly withered lemon sitting on a shelf in front of her eyes.

"I knew I saw you!"

She took it out from the fridge, cut a big slice, put it into the cup and filled it with hot water. Lifting the cup to her nose, she inhaled the hot citrus aroma.

"Not exactly coffee, but... anything for the sake of health," she mumbled and took a sip.

She turned off the lights, walked to the French doors leading to the back garden, and stood there for some time, aimlessly staring into the darkness outside and listening to the sounds of the night. A fox barked somewhere close, in one of the neighbouring gardens. Immediately she heard a response from the garden to her right. There was a soft noise and rustling of the bushes and then the white tip of a fox tail appeared in the dark. It cautiously made its way through her garden towards a small breach in the fence, leading to the neighbouring garden and disappeared behind the bush. Very soon, she heard a cheerful whimpering, scuffling accompanied by a soft growl and low barks.

She finished her water and put the cup into the sink. She walked up the stairs, climbed under the covers and turned on the news channel. Fifteen minutes later, when she finally realised that she was not only not seeing what was happening on the screen, but also not registering a single word said by the presenter, she switched off the TV, turned down the light and curled up under the warm, heavy duvet.

Lying on her side, she looked out of the window. The sky was dark, the moon was waning and there was almost no light from its little white crescent. By her window, the streetlamp was shining bright, generously spattering its light in the dark of the night, through the half-closed blinds filling her room with a soft yellow glow. She lay not moving, turning the events of the day over and over again in her mind. Her memory brought up Mark's face and his cunning, crafty smile, when persuading her to come to his

Christmas party, he was kneeling in the middle of the restaurant. At that very moment she caught herself thinking, that today, despite everything that had happened, she felt alive – not a ghost-like creature that over the last few months wandered around, barely making it through the day – a real woman. At these memories, her lips stretched into a slight smile.

But as she smiled, her heart froze in fear. She feared these feelings would erase Guy's image from her memory. She closed her eyes, took a few long breaths, relaxing, and allowed the memories to transport her a few months back, into the depths of Sherwood Forest.

Little by little, the picture began to surface in her head. First, it was very blurry, as if hidden away from her, but slowly it began to clear, becoming more vivid, sharp, and bright. It was not an image of him, when she saw him last, – pale, as a ghost, barely breathing, almost dead, – the image that so often had haunted her in her dreams. No – she remembered him at the wedding ceremony, in the church – when big blue eyes full of love smiled at hers, when he looked at her as if no one else existed in the world but them, when they both felt as if the world was only created to bring them together.

In this state of half dream, she smiled at her thoughts and at his image in her memory. As her eyelids grew heavier, she hugged the pillow tighter and very soon fell asleep. For the first time since her return from Medieval England she didn't cry herself to sleep, she was not chased by monsters or visions of blood and death.

For the first time in many months, she dreamed of happiness.

800 Years Apart

Next morning, she woke up to the smell of freshly brewed coffee wafting around her house. Still half asleep, she curled under her soft duvet and turned to the side.

Her eyes flung wide open when she saw a glass of water standing on the nightstand. It was not there when she went to bed last night. Christine propped herself on one elbow and quietly listened to the sounds in the house. There was someone downstairs, in the kitchen. She sat on the side of the bed and at that very moment noticed a post-it note written in Mark's handwriting placed on the nightstand right under the glass of water. "Drink me" said the note.

She smiled, reached for the glass, and brought it up to her nose. The liquid smelled of lemon. She got up from the bed and drunk the water, then put on a fleece pyjama top, warm socks and walked downstairs.

"Morning, my dear," she heard Mark's voice from the kitchen.

"Morning. What are you doing here?" she asked a little rough.

"Did you sleep well?"

"Yes, as a matter of fact, I did," she said, "but you didn't answer my question. What are you doing here?"

"I brought your car. Remember, you left it yesterday at the hospital–,"

"Of course, I remember." She shot a quick glance towards the entrance, as if hoping to see her vehicle through the closed door. "I mean, what are you doing *here*?"

"I am cooking you breakfast. Hungry?"

"No. I–,"

"I promised Rup to make sure you get plenty to eat and drink."

"Well, that's very sweet of you, but how the hell did you get in?"

"Oh! I still have the keys," he patted his pocket and grinned.

"What? You had them all this time?" she stared. Mark smiled widely at her. "Hand them over!" she reached forward.

Mark caught her hand and brought her into his arms.

"Hey-hey, such a change since yesterday! I like it," he said, smiling cunningly. "And all just because you had a good night sleep. Imagine what's gonna happen after I feed you breakfast!" he winked, releasing her from his embrace.

"Oh, stop it, Mark," she said, regaining her ground and moving away from him.

"Did you drink your water?" he asked suddenly serious.

"Yes."

"Good girl!" he studied her face for a while, then picked up her hand and measured her pulse. "Feeling ok?"

"Yeah."

He stared at her face very intensely then touching her cheeks lightly turned her face to the left then to the right, then pulled her lower eyelid and asked her to look up, then down, then touched her neck and checked her glands.

"Stick your tongue out," he asked finally.

"Oh, for fuck's sake, Mark!" she pushed him away and walked into the dining area and plopped on to a sofa.

"I was just teasing you. Wanted to see how long you could withstand this torture," he laughed out loud. "Surprised, you didn't tell me to fuck off sooner."

She made a face that comprised all the words she wanted to say to him at that very moment. Mark laughed out loud. She softened a little and smiled back, gifting him one of the smiles that she so often used in a court room – wide and open it seemed friendly but with a hint of "know your limits" sent to an opponent.

He brought her a cup of coffee. She took it and took a sip – it was hot, no milk, no sugar – just the way she liked it. She relaxed on the sofa, while he talked about his work and his dad, the previous evening and upcoming Christmas. She looked at him, tentatively listening to what he was saying, yet in reality, she drifted in her own thoughts, not hearing a single word that came out of his mouth.

"… next Friday?"

She jerked her head and mumbled something inaudible in reply, got up from her seat and walked off.

"You have not heard a single word I said, have you?" Mark followed her into the kitchen. Christine looked at him bluntly. "You haven't, have you?"

"Of course, I have! No. No, I haven't. Not a single word. Sorry, too many things on my mind."

"That's ok," he took her hand gently into his and looked into her eyes. "You will let me know, if you'd want to talk about anything, right?"

"No… Yes… No! Everything's fine," she pulled her hand from his, taking a defensive position, trying to crawl back into the shell she was so comfortable in until the yesterday evening.

"Anything," he insisted.

"Thank you. If I'd want to talk, you'd be the first to know. It's just at this moment, I feel like I don't want to talk to anyone. Let alone see anyone."

"Do you imply that I should get out? Well, you won't get rid of me that fast, my lovely," he smiled. "First, I must make sure you eat breakfast and then I will leave you in peace."

He led her to the dining table, helped her into the chair and retreated to the kitchen.

"Want another coffee, while I sort out the food?" he asked putting two slices of bread into the toaster.

"Yes, please," she said automatically and turned around.

In his dark slacks and light blue polo shirt he looked very handsome. Short sleeves revealed his toned arms. She lowered her gaze.

"Such a great ass!"

Mark shot a quick glance back at her and caught the direction of her gaze.

"Enjoying the view?" He looked at her sideways. The same arrogant smile decorating his face.

"Handsome bastard," she mumbled quietly.

"I heard that!"

"Yeah-yeah," she rolled her eyes.

"You know, I like it when you're like this," he smiled, placing a cup of coffee on the table before her.

"Like what?" she looked up at him.

"Like this!" he smiled back.

"Sarcastic bitch?" she arched an eyebrow.

"Yeah!" Mark chuckled. "Then again, sarcastic bitch is so much better than a miserable cow!"

"Oh, shut your face!"

He laughed out loud and returned to his task, while Christine sat quietly at the table, consumed by her thoughts.

"There you are, my lady," Mark said, placing the plate on the table before her.

She lifted her eyes up to him, the expression on her face of pain and sadness.

"Never call me like that! Do you hear me? Never!" she cried out, all of a sudden.

"Erm, sorry. I didn't mean. Sorry. Right."

She smiled faintly, her face softening. She lowered her eyes to the plate and then lifted them up again with the same playful expression she had few moments ago. She knew Mark had noted her sudden mood swings but hoped he wouldn't bring the topic up again.

"Yum!" she murmured biting into a toast topped with mashed avocado and a poached egg.

"Glad you like it. Guess it's better than most of the stuff you've been eating lately."

Through another bite, she answered something inaudible. Finishing the toast, she swallowed her coffee and leaned back in her chair.

"Thank you, that was delicious!"

"Pleasure. It warms my heart to see you like this. Back to your normal-self, I mean. It really does."

"Is it just your heart that's getting warm?" she said, squinting at him, a little naughty smile, played about her lips.

"Well..." he hesitated for a moment. "Not just my heart! One particular part of my body is getting over excited."

Christine exploded with laughter.

"Jokes aside," he walked around the table and sat on a chair next to her. "There is something that we... that I... Christine, we can't go on like nothing happened."

"Why?" she asked calmly tilting her head to one side.

"We were close..."

"We still are," she said. "In fact, very close." She pushed her chair, moving away from him.

"You know exactly what I mean," he said, taking her hand into his, once again. "We were about to get married!"

"Engaged," she corrected.

"Yes. Sorry. Engaged. Still, you know what I mean."

"Yes, I do," she said, still the image of calmness but her breathing quickened. "We were about to get engaged. We made plans. And then you went and fucked your secretary and... and, as it turned out, have been doing that for months before you got caught."

"I was an idiot! I made a terrible mistake. I can't bear the thought that you hate me."

"I don't. Hate you," she said with a soft smile. "Not anymore, anyway. I was hurt and angry at first, but then something wonderful happened to me."

"So, you are not angry with me?"

"No," she shook her head. "And to be completely honest, I'm glad. Because of what happened, I met the most amazing person," she said, the tears looming in her eyes. "I know, I'll never see him again, but what we had between us in that short period of time, what I felt for him, was so much stronger than anything I felt before."

"I understand," he nodded. "I guess it will be stupid to ask... Do you think... Do you think we might still have a chance together? You and I. Considering, of course, you'll never see that man again."

She looked at him softly and leaned forward. Her hand touched his cheek and then slid down. Her long slender fingers dug into the collar of his polo-shirt as she pulled him closer. Mark looked at her, there was again that familiar mischievous glow in her eyes. Her face was close, her lips brushed lightly against his cheek, her cheek pressed against his. Her breath ran into his neck. She then looked at him again. Mark tensed in anticipation.

"No!" she said with the same mischievous smile.

"Gosh, you almost fooled me, but... we are still friends then, right?"

"Of course!" she laughed and kissed his cheek.

"Good! I hope you haven't changed your mind."

"What about?" she looked at him confused.

"Going to the party, of course, you, silly head!"

"Oh, seriously? Are we talking the Christmas party again? Do I really have to go?" she laughed.

"Here we go again," he rolled his eyes. "Yes, you do!"

"Oh God!" she breathed out heavily.

"It'll be fun! Black and white masquerade ball!"

"Even worse!" she added looking a little scared. "The Ball!"

"Masquerade ball," he corrected. "Behind the mask you can pretend and be anyone you want.

"Can I just be me and not go? Or, I know, even better, pretend that I did go and not–,"

"Chicken!"

"Yes!" she nodded her head vigorously. "Exactly so! Call me a chicken or whatever you like, but please do not make me go."

"Why so sudden change? You agreed yesterday."

"I only agreed so you can stop embarrassing yourself, and me for that matter, when you were kneeling on the floor in the middle of the restaurant."

"C'mon!"

"Don't want to spoil it for everyone else, really. Right now, I am not the best company for social gatherings."

"And you never will be if you shut yourself from the world! It's not healthy. And this I tell you as your friend, as well as a doctor."

"I am busy!"

"Really? What important appointments might you have on Christmas Eve?" he raised an eyebrow.

"I have nothing to wear!"

"Rubbish! What about that dress we bought in Paris? Black and white lace," he made a dreamy face. "You look very sexy in it."

"Sexy is the last thing I want to look right now," she protested.

"You are a young and beautiful woman! You should look and feel sexy 24/7."

For all her excuses, he had a counter argument. She was ready to give in.

"C'mon, say yes. You've been a miserable cow for the past five months. Time to have some fun."

"Alright, I'll come!" she uttered, got up from the chair and walked to the kitchen.

"Smashing! I'll text Rup to tell him you are coming. He'll be on cloud nine," said Mark reaching for his phone. "Now, shall we go upstairs and try your dress?"

"Wha?!" she turned sharply on her heels. "I think it's time for you to leave," she added barely able to contain a smile.

"Did I overstay my welcome?"

"Get out!" Christine laughed and pointed to the door.

*****

Mark continued to visit her every day, making sure that she had enough of fresh fruit and juices and that her fridge was stuffed with healthy food, but most importantly, to make sure that she was feeling better and actually ate and drunk what he had been supplying her with.

Feeling responsible for her physical and emotional state, he didn't want to leave her alone for long. They spent long hours together, talking mostly about current affairs and her work. Neither of them brought up Philip or the causes of her prolonged absence. She looked better and seemed friendlier and livelier, yet he couldn't judge whether that was real.

On Tuesday, at 10:00am sharp, he knocked on her door.

"Hello, you!" he smiled widely, as Christine, still in her pyjama, hair untidy after the night, opened the door.

"Oh, gosh! It's you again," she stepped away letting him in. "I thought you were a postman."

"In a way," he winked and took off his shoes. "I could be anyone you want, love, if you'd meet me like this every day."

He surveyed her – bare shoulders, with only a small strap running across them, full round breasts, and slightly aroused nipples, visible through the thin fabric of her cami. The lustful look in his eyes made her blush.

"Oh, stop looking at me like that," she mumbled and pulled a hoodie over her thin camisole.

He kissed her on the cheek, strolled into the kitchen and began to unload the groceries.

"I guess you have not eaten, then?" he asked looking around the kitchen.

"No, I haven't. Didn't feel like it," she said climbing up onto a chair and pulling her legs up. "And then, again, I knew you'll come over anyway and feed me some culinary delights. So why bother?"

"Very funny! You know, you are hilarious," he chuckled softly.

Mark put the kettle on, found a small frying pan in one of the drawers and laid bread, butter, ham, and cheese on kitchen table. Christine watched him as he cooked.

"You know, I can get used to it," she said as he placed a plate with grilled sandwich before her.

"You just have to say the word, my lady," he smiled and mimicked a bow.

Christine glared at him, in warning. There was the sharp intake of her breath, as she was about to say something, but just in a fraction of a second it all passed and she, again, was looking up at him, smiling softly.

He waited for her to finish her toast and coffee before resuming the conversation on a completely different subject.

After breakfast, while Christine was cleaning up the table, Mark brought in his kit from the car. In the last few days, this became their routine. Christine didn't complain. Not voiced her complaints, that is. Her face, however, spoke all the annoyance and discomfort he had caused her. Knowing her all too well, Mark ignored her, smiling, and shaking his head while completing her check-ups.

"You, really, don't have to do it every day. Really!"

"You are my patient, don't forget that," he replied calmly. "Besides, Rup calls every day to check on you, so I'd have to report back," he added, attaching the sleeve of the blood pressure machine to her arm.

"I'm fine! Really. I promise!"

"You know, you've already said "really" like a million times within the past two minutes. Keep still, please."

She obeyed and didn't move until machine stopped beeping and the grey electronic screen produced black the numbers.

"Your blood pressure is a bit up," he said making note in his book.

"Of course! You annoy me so much!"

"Do you rest?" he asked, ignoring her another complaint.

"How can I rest, when you're torturing me with this!" she retorted.

"You, know, you are the most impossible person I have ever met."

"That's why you love me!" she made a face. "Besides, that's what makes it so much fun!" she said attempting to get up.

"Not so fast, lovely," Mark said catching her arm and sitting her back down on a sofa. "We haven't finished yet. How are you sleeping?"

"Good! Really. Really good," she produced a smile.

Although, her sleep had improved over the past few days, it was still far from perfect. She was sill waking up in the middle of the night. Her dreams were so vivid and realistic that sometimes she lost the sense of reality.

"You know, you're a terrible liar," Mark shook his head.

"What makes you think so?"

"I don't know, it's just your eyes... You can try and maintain an indifferent face but whatever happens inside you... You are like an open book. You can't pretend." At that, she mumbled another inaudible retort and tried to get up once again. "No, I'm serious, it's in your eyes. You cannot pretend."

"You'd be surprised! I'm actually very good at pretending."

"No, you are not! Well at least you can't fool me. I know you too well, to know when you lie."

"Or, perhaps, like I said another day, you don't know me at all, and only see what you're allowed to see," she looked at him, that bold, demanding stare of hers. She was now suddenly all serious. "Perhaps it's all a mask... one of many..."

"Yes, the thought has crossed my mind at some point. I always wondered how you do your work. You are completely different "in" and "out" off work."

"Same question back at you, Mark," she smiled back at him.

"No, I mean it. Sometimes, I feel like there're two different people living inside you."

"Oh, here we go! Another case study? A classic case of MID!"

"What on earth is that?" he burst out laughing.

"Multiple Identity Disorder," she said a little hesitant.

"It's DID – Dissociative Identity Disorder, professor Hawk, or MPD, if you wish. And off the record, I don't think you're crazy. No yet, anyway. However, if you don't start looking after yourself, you'll need a professional help. And much sooner than you think."

"I know," she said quietly. "It's just too much. Too much of everything."

"You know, I'm here for you, if you need me... for anything," Mark took her hand in his.

"Yes, I know. Thank you," she sighed, patting the back of his hand.

"Right, shall we get back to my original question then?" he smiled. "How is your sleep?"

"Ok, I guess... When I sleep, that is," she smiled wearily. "I find myself sometimes lying in bed for hours, staring out of the window or at the dark ceiling. I get restless, drowning in the endless sea of thoughts. After a while, I kinda black out and don't know what happens, when I'm back again it's already morning."

"How long have you been like that?" he asked concerned.

"Past five month."

"What? No wonder you collapsed. You're exhausted! You need rest! And sleep! Hours and hours of sleep."

"That's the point, I don't feel like sleeping. My dreams haunt me!" she cried desperately.

"Ok, I think I know what you need," he pulled out a prescription paper from his bag. "I can prescribe you something, to help you sleep."

"I don't need a sleeping pill, Mark."

"It's not a sleeping pill, it a natural hormone that your body produces when it's time to sleep. It'll help you to relax and sleep. Most of my patients say after taking it, they sleep better, and their dreams become more colourful and vivid."

"I don't want my dreams to be more vivid or colourful than they already are!"

"Well, perhaps, you'll be among the minority, who do not get any dreams, just a good night sleep," he said and began to write.

"Ok, I might try it later," she agreed and put the prescription on a dining table.

"By the way I met Monica today, on the way here," Mark said, feeing the need to change the subject.

"Oh really, how is she?"

"That's exactly what she asked me. She said she hadn't seen you for a few months."

"Yeah, I know. I didn't feel like going there," Christine said a little tired.

"Why not? I thought you loved riding and that animal... what's its name?"

"Richie?" she smiled. "He's gorgeous and I do love riding. I just don't feel like it."

"Right. We'll need to do something about it as well. You're clearly suffering from depression–,"

"Yeah! Well, maybe, you can prescribe me another pill, doctor!" she cut him off and finally got up from the sofa.

"Maybe I will!" he retorted. "You're being impossible."

"Who is being impossible? I told you, Mark, I've been very busy with work, too many things on my mind, I'm just tired, and don't want to see anyone."

"My sentiments exactly," he said, speaking a lot calmer. "You've been exhausting yourself! You need rest, good sleep and fresh air."

"Ok, doctor, I promise, I'll go for a walk later today. Maybe, will pop into the school and say hello to Monica," she made a sweet face.

"I know you wouldn't but pretend that I believe you," he smiled.

She did not reply.

They spent more time talking about nothing in particular, until Mark's phone rung. He walked into the hall, and, after spending about five minutes on the phone, answering to the person on the other line in short quick phrases, returned to the kitchen and quickly packed his bag.

"Is anything the matter? Is it about your dad?" Christine asked worried.

"No, all good," he answered shortly. "But as much as I enjoy your company, I need to go now. See you tomorrow," he said kissing her cheek.

"Tomorrow? I think my fridge is loaded with food. You don't really have to come in again tomorrow. I'll behave, and even go for a walk, I promise.

"You've forgot, haven't you?"

"Forgot about what?" she stared at him.

"Christmas Party… The masquerade-ball!" he laughed.

"Oh, dear god!" she issued a muffled grunt.

"You promised! You have to come," Mark would not listen to her excuses and cut her off before she was able to voice yet another complaint. "We already had this conversation. You are coming, even if I had to drag you there myself and then tie you to a chair, so you won't run away!"

Laughing out loud, she raised her hands in surrender.

"All right! Fine!" she said pushing him out of the front door. "See you tomorrow."

*****

The morning of the next day she spent preparing for the party.

After fixing herself a quick breakfast, she took the dress out from the wardrobe and hung it in the garden to air.

Although the forecast predicted rain and even snowstorms towards the end of the day, the late December morning was very mild, yet still a bit cold for one who decided to venture outside, wearing only their pjs.

After issuing two loud sneezes and receiving a wish of good health from behind her neighbour's fence, she realised, she was probably too adventurous in the choice of her clothing and quickly changed into a jeans and a thick knitted jumper. She made a fresh cup of coffee and went to sit in the garden. Basking in the warm rays of the golden sun, she enjoyed the quiet and calmness of the morning, feeling the fresh breeze ruffling through her hair. Listening to the birds happily chirping in the trees, she watched as the light fabric of her dress billowed with each new gentle gust of the wind.

She looked into the blueness of the high sky and then closed her eyes and leaned back in a chair. Immediately, her mind produced Guy's image. It was that very day when hiding from the scalding sun, he and his men took refuge under the canopy of the blacksmith's forge – his black shirt tucked under his belt, his broad bear chest covered with small droplets of sweat that sparkled in the sun as precious gemstones, his dark wet hair hanging over his forehead and his deep blue eyes...

She smiled to herself wondering what he was doing exactly at this moment. How was he? Was he alive? Was he well? Was he in Locksley or in Nottingham? Was he preparing for Christmas? Was he alone or...?

As much as she tried not to think about it, the last thought has been haunting her for some time now.

A gust of wind came out of nowhere. She shivered and, as if waking up from a daydream, she looked around, trying to figure out where she was. She was at home, she was alone.

She looked up. Where just moments ago – before she wandered off in her thoughts to meet with him again – there was an endless blue of a winter sky, now sat dark grey clouds chased in by a strong northerly wind.

Christine took a long sip of her long cold coffee, picked up her mug and returned to the house. She tried to stop herself from thinking about Guy, as it didn't provide any comfort to her bleeding heart, and only made the wound deeper and feeling of the pain sharper and stronger. She picked up a book from a shelf and cuddled up on the sofa in a vague attempt at occupy her mind.

It wasn't long before she realised that she was reading the same line over and over again, making absolutely no sense of the words that stared back at her from the white page. She put the book away and turned on the news. She watched as the pictures changed before her eyes, she was trying so hard to hear what the presenter was saying that her head began to hurt. She switched off the TV, poured the reminder of the cold coffee into the sink, and made herself a fresh cup.

Slowly sipping the hot strong liquid, she watched through the window as the wind whirled stray leaves in a magical, slightly sad, waltz of a dying nature. It picked them up and spun mercilessly high above the ground, then retreated, letting leaves to descend, as if allowing them to take a short quick breath before picking them up again and sending them spinning in a chaotic motion.

She was about to gulp down the remainder of her drink when the dark clouds, brought in by the strong winds, opened and harshly emptied their contents.

"And here comes the promised rain..." she mumbled, finishing her coffee.

She walked away from the window before rushing back and out of the garden door. As quick as she tried to be, she was no match for the forces of nature, and within a short period of time her dress soaked though till the last tread.

"I guess I do not have to go now..." she said strangely relieved.

She hung the dress in a utility room, placed an old towel underneath it to catch the dripping water and was about to go upstairs to dry her hair when her phone rang.

"You no longer hide your number!" she greeted the caller.

"Well, now as we are back on speaking terms, I thought it's more likely you'd answer, knowing it's me," Mark chuckled softly. "Tell me. You didn't hang your dress outside this morning, did you?"

"How did you guess?" she laughed.

"I told you, I know you too well! How bad is it?"

"Ruined!"

"That was expected," he answered calmly. "Right. There are dry cleaners a few blocks away from you. They do two hours expedited service. I'll message you their address now–,"

"You don't give up, do you?"

"You know, I don't, so, don't argue. Please. Knowing you, I already called them and said that a desperate lady might pop by with a ruined dress that requires some urgent TLC. They said they'll do it. They open till 4pm."

"Gosh... I guess I'll have to come up with some other excuse–,"

"No excuses accepted, love."

"Even if they do fix the dress, you said it's a masquerade ball and do not have a–,"

The doorbell rang.

"Hang on! Someone's at the door."

She dropped the call, tucked the phone into the back pocket of her jeans and walked to the front door. As she opened the door, she saw a big UPS van parked outside her house. A tall, good looking man with a ginger beard dressed in a uniform, quickly handed her a long box, made her sign for the delivery and having wished her a happy Christmas in a strong New Zealander accent, got back into the truck, and drove away.

Christine walked back to the kitchen and placed the box on the table. The phone in her pocked made a distinctive noise. She took it out and looked at the screen.

"Were you trying to say something about not having the mask..." said the line that ended with a smiley face.

Christine stared at her phone, then at the box then at the phone again. She opened the box. Inside there was a beautiful crimson rose and a small box with a black mask made of delicate lace with two long ribbons attached to its sides.

Her phone buzzed again. This time the message consisted only of a question mark and emoji face stretched into a wide grin.

"You're a sneaky bastard!" she typed-in quickly.

"I told you no excuses will be accepted. Do you like it?"

"Yes! It's beautiful."

"Then say you'll come. Please."

She didn't reply.

"Please," came a message and moment later another one. *"Pretty please..."*

The next message made her giggle. It was a picture of Mark trying to adopt an angelic face, his hands folded on his chest in prayer.

"Pretty please..." read the message.

About a minute later came in another message that made Christine burst out laughing. It was a picture of Mark, hands still folded, still trying to maintain an angelic composure and balance a jar of cherry jam on his head.

"With a cherry on top?" Christine messaged back.

Her phone rang, she answered, still laughing.

"So, is it a "yes" then?" Mark asked through her giggling.

"Yes!"

"Perfect! Do you want me to pick you up later? About six-ish?"

"No. I'll drive."

"Is your car ok? I remember you mentioned something was wrong," he asked.

"Nah. It's just a seatbelt, keeps unbuckling all the time. Will take the car to the garage after the break."

"Alright. I'll text you the address. Don't forget to sort out your dress. I'll see you later! It's gonna fun, you'll see."

"Bye," she said in her most charming voice and dropped the call.

*****

The rain had stopped and bright sun, once again, took over the blue sky. She took her dress to the cleaners and then, for three hours, wandered about the empty streets of her little area, making use of Mark's suggestion to get some extra dose of fresh air and to clear her head.

She popped into a corner shop at the top of the road and picked up a Christmas card. Having carefully written her apologies for not being in touch and finishing her message with the best wishes of health and prosperity she walked to the riding school and posted the card through the letterbox of the school's office. She knew the school would be back, in early January.

She took a little stroll in the park, walked to the cafe, and was surprised to find it still open for business. A cup of coffee in hand, comforting herself that she was already in the park, Christine decided to visit the clearing.

The enormous oak that six month ago had opened for her a secret passage and turned her life upside down, taking her to a completely different reality, changing her existence forever, was still there. It had dropped its leaves and the ground around it was all covered with acorns mercilessly munched by park inhabitants, but even so, it took her breath away. She walked around the tree, her hand gliding across the massive trunk. With a soft sound the dry bits of bark crushed under the pressure her fingers and slowly descended to the ground. Christine walked into the opening on the other side of the tree. Surprisingly, it felt very warm and dry, there was no dampness that prevailed outside, after the rain.

She stopped in the middle of the tree. Her mind once again brought back memories of him. Out from the darkness of the tree, he looked at her, his sky-blue eyes filled with love were smiling tenderly, gleaming with a soft light. Her heart pounded in her chest, returning the feelings that she had been trying to silence for the past five months, making them even stronger. Too painful to bear. No matter how much as she tried to persuade herself that it would get better eventually, in her heat she knew she would never forget him.

Christine closed her eyes, squeezing them tight, and drew a sharp breath, trying to steady her rushing heart. She opened her eyes again and there, right before her, she saw a ball of light. A very small, faint, merely a vision, but she knew it was there. It was real – not another product of her imagination. She could feel its presence. She gasped for air as her eyes began to water – the sphere of light was too small and to faint for her to cross over.

She outstretched her hand. Glimmering in the colours of the spectre, the light sphere landed on her palm.

"I wish... I wish I could share this day with you..." she muttered, swallowing her tears. "Merry Christmas, my love. Please know, wherever you are, I love you still."

As soon as she said these words, the light had disappeared, as if sucked into the black hole, as if it was never there. Only the soft silver shinning echoing in her eyes reminded her of it. She wiped the tears away and walked out of the tree. The sun was still shining in the sky, but air had become noticeably colder. Driving the sad thoughts away, she quickly walked further and further away from the tree and out of the park.

*****

She picked up her dress from the cleaners and returned home to get ready for the party. She took a shower, styled her hair, and put the dress on. Mark was right when he said the dress made her look sexy. For a long time, she studied her reflection in the mirror. Having shut herself from everything, she almost forgot how fulfilling it was to feel beautiful and desired.

She went through the box with her jewels, looking for something appropriate for the occasion and took out a silver ring with amethyst setting, the one that Guy gave her on the day of their trip to Gisborne, on the day when the Sheriff returned from London. She often wore it at home and fell asleep with it on her finger, but never before she had worn it out in the public. She slid the ring onto her right ring finger, picked up a small clutch bag and went downstairs.

She packed her phone and her bank card into her clutch bag and sat on the second step of the staircase to put the shoes on. She fiddled with the lacing of her heels for some time, then got up and walked to the kitchen and back. No way she would be able to drive a car in those! She sat on the step and untied the laces. Elbows pressing into her knees, chin resting on the palms of her hands, she looked around surveying the stand that hosted her shoes, trainers, and boots. Nothing seemed appropriate for the occasion or for the dress she picked. Eventually, her eyes stopped on a pair of her old and shabby DMs. A cheeky smile appeared on her face and slowly spread into a wide grin.

The Party

Christine parked a few streets away from the Dorchester hotel, and fixed the black mask onto her face. Trying not to mess up her hair, she tied the thin ribbons at the back of her head, spread long curls on her shoulders and shot one last glance into the back-view mirror.

She draped a white pashmina over her shoulders, grabbed the shoes from the back seat of her Mini, picked up the hem of her dress with a free hand and slowly began to make her way towards the hotel.

The warmth of the day still dominated. From one of the side streets, a church bell chimed eight. She walked, not hurrying anywhere, slowly breathing in the freshness of the evening. At the beginning and at the end of each street and alley shone yellow lamps, filling the evening London with a magical golden glow.

Music and cheerful voices were flowing from the windows of the houses on both sides of the street. Through the windows that were not covered with curtains, she could see the silhouettes of people with plates and glasses. Generations gathered under one roof to celebrate Christmas.

Around the corner the darkness consumed her. There were no lights in the windows of the houses and the lamp at the top of the street didn't work. From time to time it produced a low click, lit up for a few seconds and then dimmed again. Having chimed the hour, the church bell quietened, the silence descended upon the street – there was no music, no voices, no random pedestrians. Christine walked slowly, her steps echoing in the evening calm.

After a while, she saw a silhouette of a man sitting on a low brick wall separating a building from the pedestrian path.

His figure and the manner in which he sat seemed strange – his long legs were stretched across the pedestrian path, his back and shoulders slouched – and he himself looked a little uncomfortable and awkward, as if he was a mythical giant, a Gulliver, that suddenly appeared in this country of little men and now, unsuccessfully, was trying to blend into his little surroundings.

The red light of his cigarette lit up each time his hand rose to his lips. Realising it was too late for her to turn back, Christine lifted her eyes up and, trying to pay him as little attention as possible, slowly walked in his direction. As she walked past him, the man, all of a sudden, lifted his hand up and saluted to her in a military manner.

"Good evening," he said in a heavy American accent.

Christine didn't reply and continued on her way, walking away from him, faster than she originally intended.

She had already moved down the street when she heard, as the man got up from his seat and walked after her.

"Not." he said, catching up with her.

"What "not"?" she asked, not really sure why, and turned to face him.

"Not drunk."

"I didn't say you were," she said with indifferent face.

"Didn't have to," he replied, tired. "It's all clearly written on your face, despite it being covered by this charming little mask. Not drunk. Jet lagged."

"If you say so. Good evening," she said politely and turned to leave.

"Wow!" the stranger exclaimed as Christine took her first step. His eyes fixed on to her feet. "Only a very self-confident woman could wear boots like that with a dress like this!"

Christine chuckled, stopped, and turned to face him once again.

"A self-confident woman can wear anything she wants without worrying what anyone might think."

"True!" he flashed a bright smile.

"Besides," she added a little coquettishly. Her eyes smiled under the mask. "My grandma always said that confidence is the sexiest thing a woman could wear."

"Oh, I love your grandma!" the man laughed out loud. "Is she still alive?"

"Very much so!" Christine lied, getting into the spirit of the game. She never knew her grandmother but at that moment it did not seem important. Two strangers on Christmas Eve, on the dark streets of London – details seemed insignificant and unimportant. "She lives at her country estate, in Derbyshire."

"Country estate?!" he asked, still smiling broadly. "I have a feeling that her estate includes a huge Manor, a few thousand acres of forest and other lands, perhaps?"

"Precisely so! And don't forget about the lake."

"Aha, the lake! How could I forget about the lake with charming little duckies! And, may one presume, that the name of your grandma is Lady Catherine de Bourgh?"

"The very one!" Christine smiled from behind her mask.

The stranger laughed out loud once again, flashing his white even teeth in the dark of the street. At that moment Christine realised that he wasn't as awkward and odd looking as she first thought. In fact, he was very handsome. He was much taller than her, with a wide chest and broad shoulders. He was dressed in a stylish, tailored dark suit and a starched shirt so white that, in the dark, it had a soft light blue glow about it. The upper buttons on the shirt were undone, giving her the perfect view of his strong neck and muscular chest. In the chest pocket of his jacket was a small pocket square. Clean shaven, although a little ruffled, he wore a light, but very pleasant cologne.

He lit up another cigarette, walked around Christine and sat on the short wall. Making himself comfortable, he patted the brick surface, inviting her to sit by him. She smiled and walked closer, but lifted her hands, hinting to the stranger that her dress was not cut out for the purpose.

"So, where were we?" he looked up at her. "The estate, the lake, ducklings... Can one presume that the name of the estate in question is Pemberley?"

Christine nodded in reply.

"Unbelievable!" he mattered. "On the first day of my arrival, I managed to meet not only a beauty," he looked at her, as if measuring her up, a little lustfully, "but an heiress. You'll have to invite me over!"

"I can't," Christine arched her brow, still smiling sweetly at him. "It's against the rules of etiquette. A young, unmarried woman of means, cannot invite random bachelors over, even those, as terribly attractive as you."

"Of course, we're not introduced! How shocking! You, my pretty lady, go against all the rules of etiquette. Although, what could be easier..." he took another deep drag of his cigarette, got to his feet and stretched his hand out to her. "My name is J–,"

"No!" she breathed out. Her long fingers touched his lips. "No names, please."

He took her hand in his and held it for a few moments, studying her face carefully.

"You know what, I'm very jet-lagged, still haven't adjusted to your time. I only flew in from the States this morning."

"I noticed that," she said as a matter of fact.

"What? That I'm jet lagged?"

"No, that you are from America."

"Oh, that's probably my American charm."

"No, I think it's your American arrogance!"

"Can't do anything about it," he smiled widely, his eyes gleaming in the dark. "Sucked in with mother's milk. But it's not what I was meaning to say," he took another deep drag of his cigarette, rolled it between his fingers and flicked it towards the other side of the road. "I came to visit my old university friend. He invited me to his Christmas party. Somewhere around here, in a hotel," the man looked around, as if trying to determine his whereabouts. "Have not seen him in a few years, three... Maybe four... No, I guess it's three... Doesn't matter. He promised nice food and drinks and lots of pretty girls, but I can't quite make myself go. And, to tell the truth, I'd rather spend the evening in the company of this delicate English Rose," he lifted his hand and attempted to take off her mask. Christine moved her head away.

"I don't think it's a very good idea," she said, smiling playfully at him. "I'm going to a Christmas party hosted by my ex."

"Oh! How disgustingly boring!" the man exclaimed passionately and lifted her hand up. His thumb traced softly over her knuckles. "How about, we go to my buddy's party together.

Hang out there for a bit, have some food, have a little chat... finally, get rid of this annoying thing..." he made another attempt to remove her mask. "And then, perhaps, find a nice comfortable place to rest our heads for the night. I'm sure the hotel will have a lot of cosy rooms with big comfortable beds. What do you say?"

"I say, it was very nice to talk to you, Mr. Stranger, but as much as your offer is tempting, I'd have to decline. Respectfully." She freed her hand and caressed his cheek. His skin was soft and warm. "Let's not spoil it. Let our short, innocent, meeting forever stay in our memories. Two strangers met on the dark street on Christmas Eve and now part, to never meet again."

"That sucks!" he laughed and added with a wide grin, "Although, I have to admit, sounds very poetic."

"Goodbye Mr. J," she said softly, almost a whisper, turned around and walked away from him.

"At least, tell me your name," he called when Christine was already at the further end of the street.

"English Rose!" she cried over her shoulder and disappeared around the corner.

She walked another street and stopped. Her heart pounded in her chest; her cheeks burned. She just flirted with a total stranger. Someone she'd never see again in her life.

The blues that had been haunting her for so long had gone away, perhaps that was the reason she had acted as she had or, perhaps, Mark was right, she just needed to clear her head; forget about all her troubles and have fun.

Softly humming a Christmas song under her breath, she crossed the road, turned the corner, and found herself at the main entrance of the Dorchester Hotel.

*****

The venue hall was gleaming and shining brightly with the colours of gold and silver Christmas decorations. Men and women elegantly dressed in the theme of the evening – black and white cocktail dresses or evening gowns for ladies and suits for men – spread about the room, engaging in leisurely conversations, and sipping complimentary drinks. The selection of Christmas songs was softly pouring from the speakers, adding to the festive atmosphere.

As any host would do, Mark was greeting his guests at the entrance, with a firm welcoming handshake for men and brisk, fleeting kiss on a cheek for ladies, bestowing his wide friendly smile on everyone who came to share the evening with him and his colleagues. From time to time, he shot quick nervous glance at his watch. It was already past eight but there was no sign of Christine.

"Welcome my lovelies," Mark said with a slightly sly smile, as he greeted a couple of young ladies, wearing revealing little dresses, which left little to men's imagination. "The complimentary drinks are on your left, feel free–," he did not finish as a familiar figure with a black turban atop his head appeared in the doorway. "Hey, mate! Glad you came." he stretched out his hand and gave his guest a strong shake.

"Thank you for inviting me, Mark," the young doctor answered politely. "Is... she already here?"

"Nah, hasn't shown up yet. But I am confident, she will. Eventually. She promised," he re-assured him and added, with a smile, noticing a small package wrapped in silver paper, "Is this for her?"

"Yes, I thought... I might –,"

"Well played!" Mark approved. "Well played indeed! Well, come in, help yourself to the drink, food will be served at nine." he added, as new guests started to gather at the entrance.

Just when the big old clock in the hall chimed half of the hour, Mark noticed Christine making her way up the stairs.

"You are late!" he laughed.

"Everyone else is simply early," she smiled, walking up the stairs, holding the hem of her dress with one hand.

"You are not the queen!" he laughed again. "But upon my word, you are a goddess!"

Her figure was hugged tightly by the black satin of the dress, a white sash encircled her waist. Her dark curls cascaded down her open shoulder, seductively framing her high breast. The mask covered her face. She climbed the last step and then slowly glided towards him. As she moved closer to him, he saw the soft fire gleaming in her eyes, a light smile hovering about her lips.

"Wow! I expected you'd look stunning. But this!"

He outstretched his hand to her, took her slender fingers and gave her a little whirl, sizing up the way she looked from all sides before pulling her into his arms and pushing the mask off her face. "You are a goddess! Do you know that?"

"Yes. I know!" she answered with a most charming smile, as he tightened his hold of her.

As much as he tried, he was not able to resist the temptation. Seeing her looking as gorgeous as she was tonight, brought back the sweet memories of them being together. Blood rushed through his veins sending the intoxicating impulses of desire through his body.

"There's something different about you. You look... glowing... Why such a sudden change?"

71

"I just had the most interesting encounter, a block or two from here," she said pulling away from him.

"What did you do?" Mark chuckled.

"Nothing serious, just a little flirtation with a random stranger on a dark street at Christmas Eve," she said still smiling. "I guess, being a miserable cow, I forgot how good it feels to be desired."

At that he burst out laughing.

"Oh, trust me, looking like this, you'll experience a lot of that tonight," he looked at her again. "Anyway, come, let's get you a drink, food will be served in thirty minutes."

He drew her hand through his and walked her into the hall. He offered Christine complementary glass of prosecco and was about to say a toast when he heard the loud noise coming from the lobby.

"I'll be back," he said and quickly ran downstairs, towards the voices coming from the main reception of the hotel.

"... I'm afraid, we cannot let you in, if you do not know where you are going," Mark heard the manager at the front desk.

"... I'm going upstairs..." responded the harsh loud voice.

"We have several parties here tonight, Sir. Do you know which one are you going to? Do you have an invite?"

"I don't have a fucking invite!" fumed the voice. "I was invited by my friend, he's a doctor. Do you have many doctor's parties here?"

"... we have different parties here, Sir–," the manager stopped as Mark walked into the reception area through the big heavy doors.

"Jasper?!" he uttered not believing his eyes.

"Marky! My man!" the man exclaimed and added turning to the manager. "He invited me! Alright?"

"Dr?" the manager looked at Mark.

"Yes, it's ok," Mark laughed. "Thank you, Malcolm, I appreciate your help. Mr. Williams was, indeed, invited."

Mark smiled. He wrapped his arm around his old friend's shoulder and gave him a good squeeze.

"When did you land? You should've called! I would've arranged a pickup," he said, as two friends walked through the doors.

"Landed a few hours ago. Didn't want to trouble you," his friend answered with a wide grin. "Taxi took me to Oxford Street, and I wandered around for a while, trying to soak in the spirit of Christmas, if you know what I mean. It's completely different here, the spirit of the season and the other crap, you know. You can feel it in the air."

"Yeah. I know what you mean," Mark smiled, leading his friend up the stairs.

"And girls! Oh my! Who would've thought that English girls have changed so much!"

"Mm, really? I haven't noticed?"

"I met such a beauty!"

"What?" Mark laughed again. "You landed, what, a few hours ago and already picked up a girl?"

"Not just a girl, the most exquisite English Rose... she was like a vision in the night, the most beautiful woman I ever saw..."

"What have you been drinking?" Mark chuckled.

"Nothing!" Jasper raised his right hand in swear and added with a wide grin, "But you see, we were not destined to be together," he said with a theatrical sadness and pain in his voice. "She was going to some party as well. So, my life, as I know it, is ended! Therefore, I intend to get very drunk!"

"That I believe," Mark commented.

"What? That my life is over?"

"No! The you're getting very drunk bit," Mark laughed out loud. "As to your life, we'll try our best to save your miserable existence. But why are you dressed like that? Why blue? Didn't I tell you it's a black and white ball?"

"Yeah. I think you mentioned something. It might've slipped from my mind. Jetlag," he said pulling the most charming American smile.

"Anyway," Mark shook his head. "We have lots of beautiful girls here, some of them single and very willing. If you know what I mean," he added, inviting him through the doors.

"Indeed!" Jasper drawled lustfully and rubbed his hands. "Where do they serve the liquor here?"

Mark showed Jasper to the bar and, having shared with him a first shot of whiskey in celebration of their reunion, left him on a high char in the care of a bartender and re-joined his guests. At the far end of the room he saw Christine talking with Rupinder. They seemed extremely comfortable in each other's company and chatted away sharing a lot of smiles and laughter.

He was about to join them, when felt a heavy hand upon his shoulder.

"It's her!" Jasper whispered into his ear.

"What? Who?" Mark asked, as he jerked back from his peaceful reflection.

"My vision! My English rose!" Jasper said dreamily.

"Who do you mean?" Mark scanned the hall.

"There. In the corner. Talking to a dude with the funny towel around his head," Jasper whispered leaning on Mark.

"She? She's the girl you met?" Mark gasped. "Of all girls in London!"

"Isn't she gorgeous? She's even more beautiful now that I look at her."

"Isn't she just..." Mark mumbled in an unfriendly tone.

"C'mon, Marky! Just look at her!" Jasper insisted and turned Mark's head towards Christine.

"She is gorgeous," Mark breathed out, savouring Christine's form, "but... she is out of your league. Way out."

"There's no woman alive who is out of my league," Jasper declared proudly, "and you are a living witness to that!"

"I wish I wasn't," Mark muttered under his breath.

"By the end of the night, she'll be mine!" Jasper stretched his lips into an arrogant grin and made a determined step in Christine's direction. "I might even marry her!"

"What? You? Marry her?! You are the least likely person to marry anyone I've ever met!"

"Yes! But she does not need to know that, pal," Jasper winked. "C'mon, you'll introduce me."

As they walked closer Mark tried to signal to Christine, yet she was too busy enjoying herself, to notice anything around.

"Honey," he touched her shoulder.

She turned, but as she did, the smile faded from her face. In that momentary flicker of her eyes, as she noted Jasper, Mark caught a look of surprise and shock.

"Allow me to introduce you to my old university friend, Jasper Williams," Mark said. "Jasper just arrived from Boston, where he runs his own clinic," at his words, Christine's eyebrows flew up and a soft gleam entered her eyes. "Jasper, allow me to introduce you to one of the best barristers you'll find on our shores, a most charming young lady and... my fiancée. Christine Hawk," Mark said circling his arm around Christine's waist, hoping that his words and gesture would prevent Jasper from staking any further claims on Christine.

"What a surprise! Marky, you old dog!" Jasper exclaimed, taking Christine's hand in his. "Fiancé?" he gave her a long look.

"Ex- fiancée," Christine smiled sweetly at him and patted Mark's hand.

As Mark slackened his hold, she took a step towards Jasper.

"Ah, much better!" Jasper said, still holding her hand, bringing her closer. "There in the dim light of the streets, you were a mysterious beauty but now in these bright lights, you look so... confident," he declared and bent to place a soft kiss on her hand.

"And you, even in these bright lights, look so... American," she said with passion, smiling back at him.

He laughed and brought her closer, his strong arm was comfortably nesting around her waist. Her hand glided up the lapel of his jacket and stopped on his shoulder. Her face beaming.

"So, where were we?" he whispered softly into her ear, tightening his hold on her.

For some time, Mark and Rupinder stared back at them, speechless. Fighting the first shock, they made several attempts to start a conversation involving the four of them. Oblivious to their presence, Christine and Jasper were murmuring in low voices, cocooned in each other's company.

"Sorry, pal, but I was here first," Jasper declared proudly, bending towards Rupinder, and added before turning back to Christine. "Nice hat, by the way."

"Sorry, mate," Mark had pulled him aside. "There is no way you can compete with him. Come, I'll get you a drink."

He walked his colleague to the bar and shared with him a glass of strong spirit, cursing himself for ever inviting Jasper to London in the first place.

For some time, they remained at the bar talking about work and general non-consequential subjects. Occasionally, Mark looked back at Christine and Jasper, who seemed to be enjoying each other's company immensely. They smiled at one another and laughed, sharing meaningful looks. Mark felt uneasy. Knowing his university friend too well he was afraid Jasper might resort to any resources in his attempts to win Christine's favour.

Soon, the food was served and, trying to minimize the potential damage, Mark sat Christine at a table away from him and Jasper. Not that it helped. All the while Jasper and Christine exchanged long glances and as soon as the starters and the main course were done with, they found their way back to one another and carried on with their shameless flirting.

Just before the desert was served, Mark caught up with her in the hall.

"What do you think you are doing?" he asked sternly, grabbing her hand, and pulling her to the side.

"What do you mean?" she laughed back.

"You know exactly what I mean!"

"I'm having a good time," she smiled. "Wasn't that the idea of me being here in the first place?"

"Yes, but–,"

"Then what's the problem?" she arched her brow. "Don't tell me you're jealous."

"Of course I'm not jealous! But... He is dangerous!"

"Dangerous?" she repeated, her eyes wandered among the people in the hall in search of her new acquaintance. "Jack the ripper, kind of dangerous?

"No, you silly! He's not a mass murderer," Mark spat annoyed.

"What then?"

"I just don't want you to get hurt. Again."

"I know what I'm doing, Mark. Besides, I managed to survive you," she said as a matter of fact.

"Yes, but... he is worse than me!"

"Is that even possible?" she laughed. "You were pretty hardcore."

"Trust me! He's like a hundred times the worse version of me."

"A challenge!" she murmured softly and added, shooting a quick glance at the man she had been flirting with all evening. "Thank you for your concern, but I'm a big girl."

Mark was about to speak again but she stopped him, placing a finger on his lips.

"Shh, I know what I'm doing," she repeated and, in a cat like gait, moved towards her impromptu party date.

*****

When the desserts were eaten and the party guests, who were still able to keep a vertical position, gathered on the dance floor in an attempt to burn off the excessive calories of the mince pies, cheese cakes and champagne, Christine walked out to the balcony. The party hall was hot and sweaty, it smelled of roasted beef, ginger breads, and wine. The women who had come to the party with their dates were happily chatting and drinking, while those, who had come alone, were on the dance floor, moving seductively, trying to find themselves an attractive partner for the night.

Christine stepped through the double glass doors and walked towards the edge, refreshing herself with a few intoxicating, greedy breaths of the cold air. The hot steam coming from her mouth formed big, misty clouds and disappeared into the blackness of the night. She shivered as the breeze caressed her bare shoulders. After the mild warmness of the day, the night brought in a cold northern air and, up in the dark, starry skies, the clouds began to gather. Dragged in by the occasional gusts of strong wind, they moved slowly in the black heavens, gradually consuming its vastness. Christine took a long deep breath and sighed, releasing the air into the night.

Straight after dessert, her party date had moved away from her and joined two ladies, who had come to the party alone, in search of company, and were thrilled to find an easy, wealthy, as he seemed, and very handsome prey. Christine assumed it was a planned change of tactic, as Jasper attempted to provoke her jealousy. At first, she felt slightly offended, thinking that he assumed he would be able to provoke her jealousy by switching his attentions to those pathetic creatures. But as she watched Jasper flirting with them, she couldn't hold back a smile. Not more than 10 minutes had passed since he joined them, but the girls were already clinging to him, holding on to him for dear life so he would not escape their charms. He, an arm circled around each girl's waist, bringing them closer, moulding them into his body, bestowed on them his most charming American smiles.

At some point he shot a victorious glance towards Christine, triumphantly stretching his lips and he moved his eyebrows up and down. Christine smiled in return and shook her head. Silly girls. He's been playing them all along and they had absolutely no idea.

As much as their flirting was fun, while it lasted, she was happy that Jasper had decided to switch his attention to somebody else. All this began to feel overwhelming, and, having left the party inside, here, alone, in the dark of the night, she felt much better. Better and free.

Suddenly the strong scent of cigarette smoke broke into the freshness of the night. Knowing full well that smoking in the building was not allowed, Christine looked around in search of the lawbreaker. She took a step closer towards the edge of the balcony and leaned over to see if the smell could've come from downstairs, but there too she could see no one. Assuming that the smoke might have been brought in by a gust of wind from somewhere else, she was about to resume her peaceful reflection, when she heard somebody clearing their throat right behind her.

She turned sharply and squinted, trying to make out the shape out of the shadowy mass in front of her. She then saw the faint red light of a cigarette suddenly appeared, as out of nowhere. It floated up in the air and flared up bright red, illuminating the face and a bold, arrogant grin. It then dimmed, made its way down and disappeared as if it was not there in the first place.

"How long have you been here?" she asked.

"Long enough to appreciate the view," Jasper said, his eyes gleamed in the dark.

Her lips quivered involuntary. Trying to hide the smile she lowered her head but, having fought the first urge, lifted it back up and leisurely walked to the man sitting in the shadows on the windowsill.

"She walks in beauty, like the night of cloudless climes and starry skies; and all that's best of dark and bright meet in her aspect and her eyes," Jasper recited with passion as she moved closer to him. "One shade the more, one ray the less, had half impaired the nameless grace, which waves in every raven tress, or softly lightens o'er her f–,"

"You missed two lines," she interrupted him, narrowing her eyes playfully.

"Did I really?" he looked up at her, his mouth, once again, stretched into a bold grin.

"Yes, you did."

"I thought I might," he smiled again and placed his hand gently on her waist. "It's been a while since I last said these words but then I saw you walking to me like this, the words, themselves, jumped to my lips."

He looked at her and took a sharp breath. In his eyes she saw a shadow of lustful desire, like she was a delicious meal and he was a ravenous artist, ready to devour her. He smirked, circled his arm tighter around her waist, sat her down on his knee and took another drag of his cigarette. Releasing the smoke into the night, he rolled the cigarette stub between his fingers and flicked it away, over the edge.

"You know, they can kick you out for that."

"I'd like to see them try," Jasper said with the same arrogant grin, then reached into his pocket for a cigarette case, and lit up another cigarette.

He slackened his hold of her and reached to the side. At the far end of the windowsill he found his glass of whiskey and brought it to his lips.

"So, does it usually work?" Christine asked, still smiling.

"What?"

"All this romantic poetry?" she arched an eyebrow. "Do you really think you can seduce me by reading me Byron poems?"

"You? No!" he murmured softly, lifted the cigarette up to his lips and inhaled it deeply. "Any other girl there, perhaps. You – no!"

"I have to admit, I was rather touched. But Byron? You, probably, would've had more luck should you've tried to some of your, American, poets. Although, there are probably none that would compare with our, British," she smiled sweetly as she injected the insult into his American pride.

"We do have some," he replied taking another sip from his glass, "but yours are considerably better. And then, again, Byron never fails!"

"So, you have tried this before!" she laughed. "How many have fallen into the trap?"

"You'd be surprised," he grinned widely.

"Well, let's get this straight then, shall we? I'm not gonna sleep with you, no matter who you'll be reciting today."

"Oh, what a waste of a poem!" Jasper sighed disappointed. "And there I was, hoping I might get lucky today."

"If you wanna get laid, you should return to those two lovely ladies you were speaking to earlier."

"I might just do that," he got up. Christine slide down from his knee. "See ya!" he added and disappeared behind the glass doors.

Left alone and in such an imprudent manner, Christine had opened her mouth to send a retort after him, as Jasper peered back.

"Just kidding!" he laughed. "Wanted to see your face."

"Did you now?" she said, unamused.

"You are a much better prize! Besides, I love challenges," he grinned again. "C'mon, let's get a drink."

"Haven't you had enough already?"

"There's always room for one more," he smiled. "You look like you might need one too, aren't you cold? Come, my treat!" he added opening the doors for her.

"It's an open bar," she smiled stepping though the doors, into the hall.

"Even better! You can get me a drink. Double whiskey, no ice."

They walked to the bar and got their drinks, but the music in the hall was too loud for them to hear one another. After a while, Jasper offered to seek refuge in one of the reception lounges outside the hall.

"Come in, my dear," he said opening the door for Christine.

Holding drinks in both hands she walked into the room, Jasper followed her. As he closed the door, Christine heard a key turning in the lock.

"Why did you do that?" she asked, her playful mood fading away.

"So we are not disturbed," he said quietly. He walked towards her, took the glasses from her hands, and placed them on a small table by her side. "There. Much better. My rose!"

He lifted his hand and stroke her face.

"Open the door," Christine said calmly, taking a step away from him.

"I will, if you kiss me," he grinned. "Just one kiss."

"Open the door or I *will* scream."

"Good luck with that!" he smiled sinisterly.

Christine glared at him. One step at the time, she walked backwards, away from him, but Jasper had no intention of giving up his pursuit. He pulled her close, his hand, once again, was around her waist.

"C'mon, don't be like that..." he whispered into her ear, as Christine tried to push him away. "And on that cheek, and o'er that brow, so soft, so calm, yet eloquent..." he said, his fingers caressing her face.

"Stop reciting that blasted poem!" she demanded, struggling to free herself. "Let me go!"

"No!" he breathed out, pushing her back, towards the wall. "I can't let you go. My rose."

Two more steps and Christine found herself pressed against the back wall of the room. Blinded by lust and desire, Jasper wanted her there and then. He twisted her hand behind her back. He moved on her, his lips looking for hers, softly gliding up her neck towards her mouth.

Managing to free her hand, Christine pushed him away, giving him a sound slap on a face.

"Spiteful little cat!" Jasper grinned, resuming his assault.

Driven mad by urge, he pushed her harder into the wall. Restraining her hands, he placed hard, violent kisses on her lips, grabbed her hair and pulled it down, bringing her exposed neck up, closer to his hungry lips.

Desperate to free herself, she pushed him away and brought her hand up in faint attempt to punch him in a face but failed. Her knuckles barely brushed against his skin. The ring on her finger, slid across his cheek. The sharp stone had scratched his skin. Jasper groaned and took a step back.

"My rose has thorns..." he said, angrily, touching his cheek. "Let's see what we can do about that."

Wincing in pain, he moved on her once again, but she slipped between the chairs and ran for the door. With trembling hands, she tried to turn the key, but her fingers would not obey. Jasper was right behind her. Finally, as he was about to grab her hand, she managed to turn the key and swung the door open.

Rushing out of the room, she bumped into Mark.

"Christine! There you are, I was looking for you everywhere... is everything alright?" he asked seeing her state of shock, her hair all messed up, lipstick smudged, face flushed.

"No! I'm not bloody alright!" she said angrily. Taking a step away, she revealed to Mark the sight of Jasper standing in the doorway.

"Marky! What a surprise! Christine and I were just having a little fun," he smiled, trying to turn away, to hide his scratched face.

"Fun!" exclaimed Christine. "Do you call this fun?"

"What happened?" asked Mark, worried.

"Nothing, I'm telling you, just fooling around," said Jasper as he took a step towards Christine.

"You! Stay away from me!" she said angrily and moved to stand behind Mark.

"I think you need to leave, Jasper," Mark said calmly.

"What? What do you mean leave?" Jasper protested loudly. "You invited me to the party, I'm..."

"Jasper," Mark interrupted him. "I invited you to have fun, not to assault my guests. It's better you leave."

Stirred by the commotion, people began to gather in the hall.

"I'm having a great time!" Jasper protested.

"There is no need to make a scene, Jasper. You leave. Now..."

"What if I don't?"

"You don't want me to call security, do you?" Mark said, keeping calm, noting two man in black suits walking up the stairs, towards them.

"Is everything alright Dr. Laferi?" asked one of them, evaluating the situation in one short glance.

"Yes, everything is fine Markus, Mr. Williams is just leaving," Mark said looking at his friend. "If you could, please, show him the exit."

"Sir, follow us, please," one of the men said politely, moving to Jasper, ready to force him out should need be.

"Merry fucking Christmas!" Jasper shouted before turning around and making his way down the stairs.

*****

"Are you alright? How are you feeling?" Mark asked as Christine made herself comfortable on a sofa in the lounge of his apartment.

"How do you think I feel?" she looked up at him and shook her head. "It was a bad idea me coming to the party in the first place! I knew it wouldn't end well."

"You should've just listened to me and stayed away from Jasper. As I told you to," Mark gave her a fatherly look. "I told you he is dangerous."

"We were just flirting. No harm. Who would've thought he'd decide to savage me there? Besides, you said he was not Jack the Ripper kind of type, so I didn't see the problem."

"Well, if for you it was just light flirting, his intentions were obvious."

"Of course they were obvious! Do you think me an idiot? But I told him straight I wasn't going to sleep with him."

"Did you really say that to his face? That you wouldn't sleep with him?"

"Absolutely! You said yourself, you know me well, so what kind of question is that? Don't tell me you thought I would've slept with him?"

"To tell the truth, I had my doubts. For a moment. Anyway..." he paused. "Are you sure you don't want me to give you a lift?"

"Nah," she sighed, "thanks, but I'll drive. My car is parked a few blocks away. Don't want to find it clamped tomorrow. Not my idea of spending Christmas Day, trying to free a car from a compound."

"Nobody's gonna clamp your car. It's Christmas!"

"You never know!" she chuckled, pulling her boots on. Mark stared at her. "What?"

"Still can't believe you wore these boots with the dress!"

"That's exactly what your friend had said when I first saw him on the street. They're cool, aren't they?" she lifted her leg up. "Anyways. Return to your guests, I'll be fine," she got up from the sofa and collected her things.

"Wait," said Mark as if he'd suddenly remembered something and ran up the stairs.

He soon returned with a small bottle of water and a little purple bottle with pills.

"Here, take one of these this when you get home and one more 30 min after. It will help you relax and sleep," he said placing a bottle into her hand.

"Is that your magical... something, you were telling me about? I don't remember what you said it was."

"Yes," Mark smiled. "The best remedy for sleep problems. Are you sure you do not want me to call you a cab?"

"No! Can you imagine how much it will cost me? From here all the way to Kingston on Christmas Eve."

"I'll pay."

"Thank you, but no, thank you! I'll drive."

"You've been drinking."

"Just two glasses of prosecco," she lied giving him a charming smile. "I'm well within the limits."

"Then, at least let me walk you back to your car."

"This, you can do," she smiled and took his elbow, and together they headed for the door.

In the light of the streetlamps they walked, the sound of their steps echoing in the empty streets. The air smelled of burned wood and chestnuts. They got to the car and she quickly got in and started the engine. She rolled the windows down and blew him a kiss goodbye.

"Speak to you tomorrow."

"Sure," he smiled. "Buckle up!"

"Will do," she said reaching for the safety belt and, finally, managing to buckle in after the fourth attempt.

"Drive safely," said Mark leaning towards her window.

"I always do," she answered and smiled again.

"Call me when you get home, alright?"

"Yes, daddy, I will," she mocked him in return, closed the window and drove away.

She turned into Park Lane and hit the traffic. To her surprise, the streets were still busy and after spending fifteen minutes in a traffic jam at the Wellington Arch, she finally turned into South Kensington.

The streets were brightly lit with Christmas lights and the area was buzzing with life. The road was busy, shops were closed but the cafes and restaurants were still open, people were still walking around, moving from one pub to another.

As she left South Kensington and entered Hammersmith the road cleared up a little – she was able to get through two traffic lights before hitting another traffic jam. She turned on the radio and sat in the car patiently, singling along with the Christmas songs, drumming her fingers over the steering wheel.

The wind outside picked up and it started to rain. She turned on the wipers and leaned forward to better see when the light would change. It soon turned green and slowly, moving along with the rest of the traffic, she managed to get to the next red light. As the droplets of rain banged on the windscreen of her car, she realised she was feeling thirsty, and reached to the back seat for her bag. As she stretched her hand and leaned back, her belt made a soft click and slowly slid up to her chest. Christine swore quietly, wiggled herself out of the strap and brought the bag forward, placing it on the passenger seat next to her. When the car behind started to flash its lights, she realised the light had changed but she was still standing at the crossroads. Christine flashed her emergency lights, apologising to the driver behind and moved forward.

After the next intersection, she parked by the side of the road, turned on her emergency lights and reached for the bottle of water. As she took it from the bag, a little, dark purple bottle rolled onto the passenger seat. She picked it up and read the description on the back.

"Hormone produced naturally in the pineal gland at the base of the brain. Natural treatment for sleep disorder. Take one pill an hour before desired bedtime or as otherwise prescribed by the doctor."

She looked outside, then at the clock. Once she crossed the Chiswick Bridge, she would be home in about 15 minutes. She opened the little bottle, took two pills, and swallowed, sending after them half a bottle of water. After several failed attempts to fasten her seatbelt that would not stay in place no matter how much she tried, she started the engine and re-joined the traffic.

As she made her way towards the Chiswick Bridge, the rain had stopped, but as she crossed the bridge, big, soft, fluffy cottons of snowflake began to fall from the sky.

After the bridge, the road was empty, as if by the wave of a magical wand, all the cars and people around had disappeared. Taking advantage of the empty street, she pressed the accelerator down and speeded towards Lower Richmond Road ignoring the annoying beeping sound of her seatbelt alarm.

As she reached Manor Road, the snow started harder, and despite her windscreen wipers were working on full, she was barely able to see the road ahead. At the Queen's Road roundabout, she almost collided with another car that appeared out of nowhere.

Suddenly she felt very tired. Her hands and legs wouldn't obey her commands, her eyelids grew heavy. Fighting the fatigue, she pressed the accelerator pedal hard and raced her car down the Star and Garter Hill and into the Petersham Road.

The steep hill was wet and slippery. Heavy snow was falling from the sky as in the magical Christmas story, she could barely see anything, when she finally realised, she was driving with her eyes closed. The sounds around her were muffled.

As she struggled to open her eyes, the last thing she saw, were the bright lights of the oncoming car heading straight at her. An ear-piercing noise broke the air, as both vehicles tried to brake.

*****

Dr. Nick Ollman leisurely walked into his ward on the second floor of the A&E department of Kingston Hospital. He had just woken up from an quick power nap, and was ready to resume his 14-hour Christmas shift. He was one of the best doctors in the hospital, with years of experience and a passionate devotion to his profession. In the absence of a family and anyone to hurry back to at Christmas Eve, he always took charge of the night shifts over the festive period.

The clock in the hall showed five minutes past midnight.

"Merry Christmas, ladies," he said cheerfully to the girls at the reception desk.

"Merry Christmas, doctor," they replied in unison.

"Anything new? Anything urgent?"

"No. Everything is calm. Surprisingly," said the blond girl. "Jane called from downstairs reception about 30 min ago, all is quiet there as well, apart from the usual drunken and vomiting bunch and few broken noses. Nothing major."

Nick nodded, walked to the girls' desk, and sat himself on the far corner of the table.

"Seems like it's going to be an easy night," said a dark-haired girl giving him an encouraging smile.

"Never say never," the doctor answered reluctantly. "Not a Christmas we had..." he trailed off. "There is always one, reckless idiot... I am gonna get myself a coffee. You want one?"

They thanked him but refused. He got up from the desk and walked to the canteen. The night ahead promised to be long, and, as girls predicted, quiet. He would need another hit of caffeine to help him get through it.

When he got back, some 15 minutes later, he was surprised to find his calm and almost tranquil ward in of state of complete disarray. People were running back and forth, the dark-haired girl at the reception desk was talking to someone on the phone, methodically taking the notes. She replaced the receiver and up and looked up at him. Her face was pale.

"Where have you been?" she almost shouted, getting up from her desk and scooping the papers up.

"We ran out of coffee. I went to the fifth floor... What happened?"

"Seems like you were right, and we are gonna have that one reckless idiot," said the girl pushing the notes into his hands. "I'm gonna get everyone."

Nick read the notes, his face changing as his eyes scanned the papers. By the time he finished, his team had already assembled in the hall, ready for his commands.

"Incoming car crash. Female. White, Late twenties, mid-thirties. Head trauma. Deep cuts. Moderate bleeding and bruising. Potential internal injuries. Unresponsive," he finished reading the notes and walked back to the reception desk. "Prepare everything we need, get the CT scan ready."

Out of breath, one of the team ran back into the hall. Everyone looked at the nurse in nervous anticipation.

"Just got a message from the emergency unit, they will be here in about four minutes. It's snowing heavily, they cannot move faster. They are taking her straight up."

"You heard, people! Four minutes! Get ready!" Nick shouted. "Anything new?" he lowered his eyes to the dark-haired girl at the desk, who once again was taking notes on the phone.

"Yes, her name just came in. Christine Hawk, 29."

"That was fast. For a change."

"That was police. They found her driver license in the car."

"Good. Run the check to see if she has any allergies, anything we need to know and…"

He didn't finish, as another member of the team ran through the double doors of the ward.

"They are here! They are coming up through the lift on the south side."

"Shit," the doctor swore. "Try to get her relatives… but do not scare them!" he shouted as he ran through the corridor to the opposite side of the ward.

With the high-pitched ping, the doors of the lift opened, and Hell broke into the ward – people running, doctors shouting, nurses and assisting staff following the instructions in a heartbeat.

As they rolled the trolley-bed down the hall towards the scan, Nick looked into the woman's face smeared with blood. He had a strange feeling that he knew her.

The girl from the reception rushed into the room.

"Found her emergency contact info. Called the mobile and home but there is no reply. Should I call again and leave a message?" she asked trying to steady her breath.

"Who's her next of kin?" Nick asked, still trying to figure out where he'd seen the woman's face before.

"Mark Laferi. But he's not the next of kin, just–,"

"Mark! Of course! I knew I saw her before... Shit!"

"Do you know her then?" the girl asked cautiously.

"Yes, she's Mark's fiancée. Ex-fiancée."

"Mark? You mean that handsome doctor, from Brompton?" the girl said with a little blush.

"Yes! Call his work mobile, it should be in the directory," Nick cried as the girl was already speeding away from the scan room.

It was quiet in the room except for the sound of the scan and the clicking of the mouse as the doctor's assistant took notes of the readings into the medical records. The silence grew heavier as the doctors waited for the scan to finish and the results to be printed. Something that took mere minutes seemed as though it had been dragging on for hours.

"There is no answer. The phone goes straight to voice mail," the silence of the room was once again broken by the young nurse.

"Double shit!" Nick rubbed his neck. "They are having a party! Ehm... In a hotel.... what's the name... Dorchester! Call them, ask to get him on the phone. He needs to get here ASAP."

"Do you have the phone number for The Dorchester?" the nurse asked, uncertain what to do.

"Google it!" Nick shouted rushing out from the scan room with the scan printouts under his arm. "There is internal bleeding! Get her into the theatre!"

*****

As much as her work required her always be in the public eye, more than anything Christine hated to be the centre of attention. And now, of all times, after everything that had happened tonight, the only thing she wanted was to curl up under the covers of her bed and forget about everything and everyone.

There were people everywhere. In her mind, faces and voices mixed up with the strange sounds and smells. Who were all these people? What did they want with her? Why couldn't they just leave her alone?

Struggling to open her eyes, she felt powerless, numb, and lifeless. Each breath caused an excruciating pain.

A shadow appeared before her, covering what little light she could see through her closed eyelids. Someone very close called her name. They forced her eye open and blinded her with the bright light.

"... unresponsive..." she heard a muffled voice.

"What does that mean? Who's unresponsive? Why are they subjecting me to this torture?"

She felt as she had been lifted up and floated in the air, in complete darkness, then she was gently placed on something hard and uncomfortable. She heard the rattle of the metal and then whatever she was laying on moved up and forward. Then, there was a bright light, there were voices again, but she couldn't make out the words. Something was placed over her nose and mouth, her breathing become easier. After a few deep breaths, she lost the sense of reality and fell through into the darkness.

When she opened her eyes again, she found herself standing in the middle of a dark hallway. People in blue hospital scrubs were running past her, not paying her the slightest attention. She tried to speak but produced no sound, opening her mouth like a fish in shallow waters.

Right in front of her, behind the big white doors, she saw a room filled with light. Making slow unsteady steps she walked towards it and peered through the small window.

The room was charged. A sense of urgency hung about it. Doctors, their faces covered with masks, were operating in the theatre. They barely spoke, methodically making their way through the procedure. Breaking the tense silence, the machines in the room produced soft beeping and humming noises. A heap of black fabric smeared with blood lay under the operating table in a large pile.

A few moments later the monotonous beeping of the heart monitor in the room was replaced by the flat sound of death. The doctors froze for a second and a nurse, who all this time had been sitting in the corner, jumped to her feet, rushed to the wall, and pressed the big red button. The sounds of a siren took over the silence of the hall and in another instant two more people rushed past Christine and disappeared behind the big white doors.

She lingered by the door for a little longer, and then she heard music, coming from the far end of the hall. At first it was barely noticeable but with every passing second, it grew louder and louder.

"How bizarre... Somewhere in the building a party is going on like nothing is happening."

Following the music, she crossed the hall and stopped by the heavy wooden door. It was shut yet the distinctive sounds of a party were coming through strong.

She glanced back – there was nothing. In a space behind her, where, a few moments ago, she had seen people and a room filled with a bright light, there was only darkness.

Gingerly, she lifted her hand and locked her fingers around the cold metal ring of the door handle. Hesitating for another second, she pulled the door open. Familiar sounds and smells of the party gushed out to greet her. She knew this place too well.

Christine looked back at the blackness behind her and stepped forward, through the heavy doors.

Coming Soon

Sherwood Untold:
Redemption

Two years is a long time. What had happened in Nottinghamshire during this time?

What had the Sheriff been up to? Plotting and scheming, of course! And his new ally makes his ways of manipulating others so much easier.

Set in Medieval England, this book will take you on an existing journey in search for answers.

Did Guy survive his injury?

Did he remain true to his new self or does the power the Sheriff holds over him stronger than his love for Christine?

Did he, despite everything, slip back into the dark place, where he had spent the previous years?

Is there another chance for him to redeem himself?

Will her love save him once again or will his soul be forever tormented in hell?

"Redemption" is the second instalment of the "Sherwood Untold" trilogy.

The Ninth Gate Publishing
Books That Take You Places

Printed in Poland
by Amazon Fulfillment
Poland Sp. z o.o., Wrocław

63026486R00059